MARK STREET

The Intruders

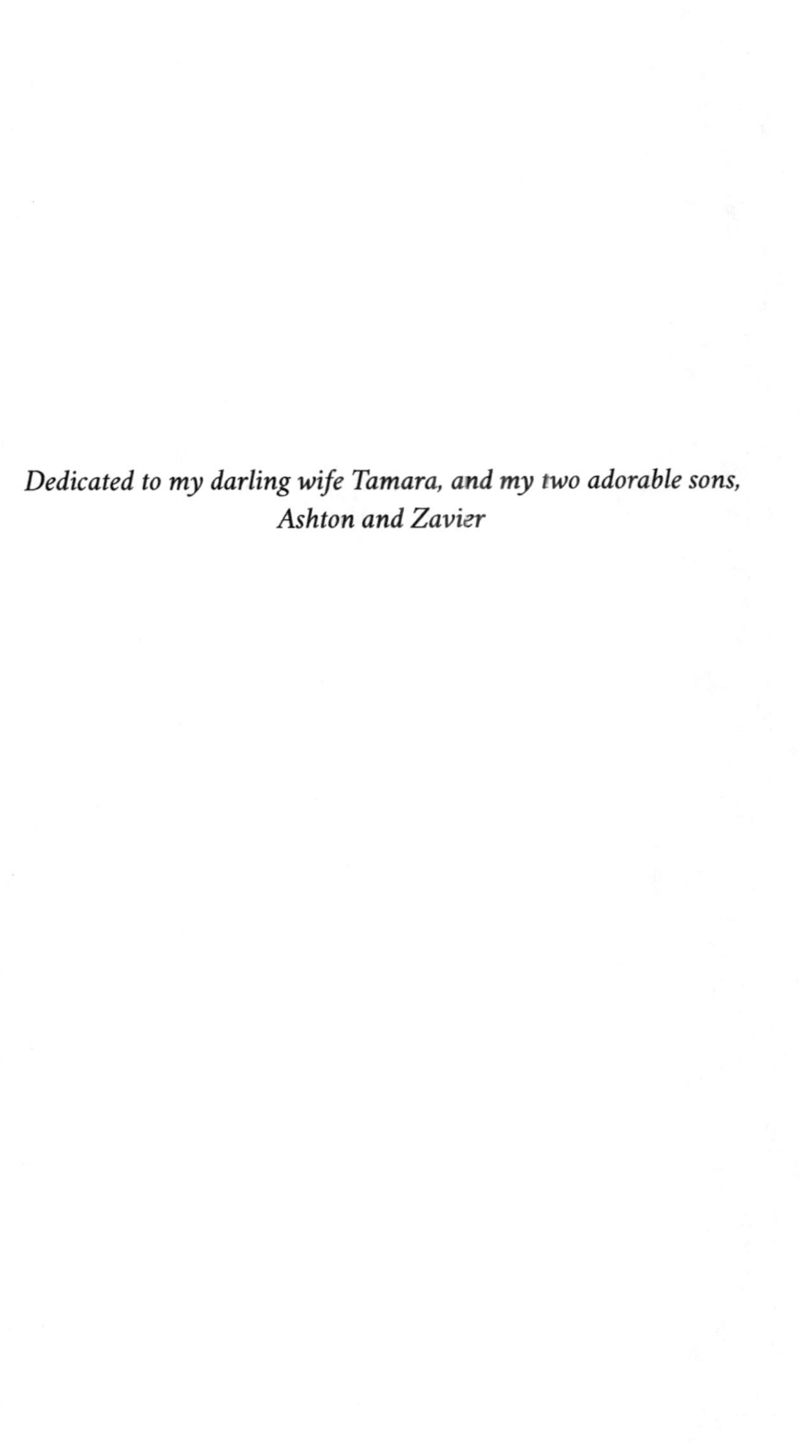

Dedicated to my darling wife Tamara, and my two adorable sons, Ashton and Zavier

Acknowledgement

I wish to acknowledge the Koa and Margany people, traditional owners of the Winton and Qulipie areas respectively.

I wish to thank Tamara Street, Julie Street, Margaret Banks, Michelle Bagley, Kerry Darnell, and Jodie Lane, for reading my drafts. Often with constructive criticism.

Thanks to Jessica Nelson who has been a wealth of knowledge and information, and who has provided me with valuable resources and contacts.

I would like to thank Dee Strange who tirelessly combed through my words and assisted me a great deal in bringing this book to see the light of day. She has been a huge source of knowledge and I thank her for distilling that information to me.

She has also kindly written the lyrics to a song, aptly titled, The Intruders. The song is available through all music platforms. An excerpt may be found here: http://www.markstreetcomposer.com

Finally, I would like to thank my endearing wife, and two wonderful boys for their incessant support.

Chapter 1

Even from the outskirts, Aurora Jemmerson could see the familiar tower of the Source-it was what kept everyone in town alive. Exiting the Trophtec Laboratory for the day, Aurora turned down Stanton Street. All the streets in Cooinda were named after notable scientists or politicians. William Stanton was a pioneer of immune system modulation, with a focus on curative treatments for various autoimmune diseases. The Cooinda government held high esteem for science and encouraged endeavours that would better the lives of its inhabitants by providing rewards to individuals that studied and worked in the field. Aurora had recently won the McPherson prize for her work on gene editing.

Aurora walked alone on the immaculate pavement towards the nearest monorail station. The people around her, all dressed in the same grey-toned suits, looked content and were busy jabbering with their companions.

"I like what you've done with your hair," she overheard one say to her friend.

"Where are we going out for dinner?" said another.

Aurora lived her life in solitude. "You don't want to hang out with other people, Aurora. Everything you will ever need is right here, at home," her mother would often say.

She'd never questioned her mother's wisdom but now she questioned herself why not. Her co-workers went out all the time. Public events came and went without her participation.

"Aurora! Wait up!" yelled Jake, running after her. His wrist device vibrated and displayed his heart rate. *160 BPM.*

Aurora stopped, allowing Jake to catch his breath. His perfectly pressed suit had not a wrinkle in it, even though he'd worn it all day and then sprinted after her. She wondered how he did it.

"Here. You left your ACCESS behind," said Jake, handing Aurora her wrist device.

"Oh, thanks," replied Aurora. "I don't like to wear it when I'm wearing gloves. It gets caught. I wouldn't get too far without it though, would I?"

Jake gave a forced chuckle. "You're leaving early today? Are you going on a date?"

"No, I have to go home. It's my birthday," replied Aurora, combing her fingers through her fine blonde hair.

"Happy Birthday."

"Thanks. Anyway, I better get going. Thanks for this," replied Aurora, fitting the device onto her wrist.

"Ok, sure. I'll see you tomorrow."

"Excuse me!" called a pedestrian, walking his robot dog.

Aurora and Jake parted to allow the pedestrian through, before walking in opposite directions.

Aurora sensed that Jake Peters had a small crush on her but wasn't sure how to respond. She hadn't had any relationships in her twenty-one years of life. Despite this, she got butterflies in her stomach every time she saw him. She particularly liked his dark brown eyes. She glanced at her wrist and selected *Emotion* from her device. *You are feeling flighty.*

Aurora shuffled onto the escalator at the monorail station. Within seconds of stepping onto the platform, a monorail appeared. As it stopped, the doors opened, and the patrons entered the carriage in an orderly procession, taking their seats. Aurora took a deep breath and inhaled the fresh filtered air. As soon as the last person entered, the doors closed abruptly and the monorail hummed out of the station towards Fairweather.

The ride's smooth cadence put Aurora to sleep within minutes. It wasn't long before she started to dream. She had visions of her standing in a beautifully manicured garden, where young children played virtual Red Rover. They looked so free-spirited. There was a large Red Cedar tree in one of the corners. She walked over to its base and stood underneath the broad canopy and admired her surroundings. She felt at peace. Her visions began to morph. The grand tree's foliage underwent abscission, leaving behind bare limbs. The lush grass underfoot was replaced with rusty coloured soil. The joyful children, now adults, were choking for air.

Aurora awoke to the monorail coming to a stop. *Thank Cooinda*, she thought to herself. *That was a nightmare.* She glanced around to make out the station name. The sign read FAIRWEATHER. She stood, gathered her shoulder bag, and made for the doors before they shut.

It was a short walk home. As Aurora turned the corner onto Princeton Street, she heard her mother clapping and calling out to her.

Jasmine Jemmerson was a lively lady. She was fifty-two years old, but could easily pass as Aurora's older sister. She had recently retired as a doctor. Nowadays, machines and artificial intelligence had replaced much of the work she had done. One's medical profile could be readily accessed by the patient's ACCESS, remotely. It detected many parameters including water content, electrolyte values, cholesterol, as well as sugar levels. It also detected heart rate, blood pressure, and emotions.

"Aurora! Happy Birthday, sweetheart," exclaimed Jasmine.

She wrapped her arms around Aurora, embracing her like a giant panda cuddling its offspring.

"Mum, ok, ok. You can let me go now," Aurora said with agitation.

Aurora attempted to pry her mum's hands off her, and slowly, her hands let go, but not before another embrace.

"Come inside, sweetheart. I'll get you dinner."

Aurora stood at the front door for a second before Nigel announced her entry. "Welcome, Aurora."

Nigel was installed in all the houses, as well as an increasing number of businesses, within Cooinda. It was a sophisticated security system that operated on the unique electroencephalogram impulses, generated by the user, through telepathy.

Aurora walked through the open door into the lounge room where she saw her father, Barry Jemmerson, watching television. "Hi, Dad."

He flicked his hand to scroll through the channels. He paused when he came to a game of soccer, playing at Cooinda's McPherson stadium. Barry was a staunch supporter of The Cooinda Crusaders. They were playing against the Cooinda Chieftains. Seeing the defeating score-line, Barry continued his channel surfing.

William McPherson was a man ahead of his time. His ingenuity resulted in the creation of Cooinda. Perhaps the most advanced feature of the city is the Source. Utilising deuteron-rich magma from below the ground, the magma is bombarded by laser, giving off heat and energy, in a process of nuclear fusion. The Source also houses large vats of potassium perchlorate that are heated and provides Cooinda with an abundant supply of fresh filtered air. Providing light, day and night, the Source allows our plants to grow, allows us to see, and sets out circadian rhythms. Ever wondered where our crisp, tasty water comes from? The Source taps into underground water basins, where it is then filtered and delivered around the city. It provides the nourishment that our plants need.

"Barry! Are you watching the history channel again?"

Barry didn't respond. He was too enthralled with his viewing.

Barry was a retired horticulturist. He held more interest in his plants than he did his family. He hadn't always been like this. Barry's persona had changed a great deal after the accident. He had no recollection of this. Jasmine did, however.

"Honey! Aurora is here," exclaimed Jasmine.

"It's ok, mum, I'll just go to my room." Aurora was exhausted. She had worked over fifty hours the past week at the lab. Many of her colleagues could not comprehend how she was so dedicated to her work, for they preferred a much more flexible lifestyle, only working twenty-hour weeks.

"No, it's not," said Jasmine. "Alright, Barry!" she yelled. "Today is Aurora's birthday, and I want you to show her some respect."

Barry called from his armchair. "Happy Birthday, Aurora." Having paid his respects he resumed channel surfing.

Jasmine grunted and walked into the kitchen. "What would you like for dinner?"

"I don't mind," replied Aurora.

"How about vegetable lasagne?"

"Sounds good."

Jasmine walked over to the counter and pressed a button on the 3D printer and announced, "Make vegetable lasagne." Within seconds, the machine came to life. Its internal arms grabbed the ingredients required from its inbuilt cabinet and refrigerator and mixed them before creating its art. The dish was then heated and within a few minutes, the meal was ready to be served.

"Dinner is ready," smiled Jasmine. She took the heated dish from the printer and placed it on the table, serving up for two.

Delicately cutting through the pasta, Jasmine asked, "So how was your day, sweetheart?"

"It was ok," replied Aurora, licking the béchamel sauce from her fingers.

"How is Jake?"

"He's good."

Aurora didn't know a great deal about Jake, other than his favourite pastime was ice hockey.

"What did you talk about?"

"Mum. I don't know," exclaimed Aurora. 'Can we change the subject, please?"

"Sure, dear. What would you like to talk about?"

Aurora pondered for a minute whilst poking her fork into a slice of potato.

"Do you think dreams are real?"

"Dreams?"

"Yeah, do you think that it's maybe us travelling to another world or another dimension?"

Jasmine chuckled. "That's pretty deep, dear. What made you think of this?"

"I don't know. I've been having these strange dreams lately. I get these visions of things that don't exist here. It's almost as though I've seen them before. It just got me thinking. What if the world we're in now isn't real. What if it's all our imaginations and there's another world outside of Cooinda?"

She noticed her mother choke on her broccoli floret before taking a sip of water. It eventually made its way into her stomach, but not without effort and considerable discomfort. "Are you ok?"

"Ah, yes. Just went down the wrong way. What do you mean, dear?"

"I mean, surely we aren't alone in this city? Surely there must be life outside of here?"

"Why would you think that? Besides, there is nothing else out there, Aurora."

"You seem very certain."

"Many people have asked the same question that you have, you know?"

"And?"

"And what? They've come to the same conclusion that I have."

"But why?"

"Because there's been no proof otherwise."

"Has anyone attempted to explore?"

"Aurora!" exclaimed Jasmine, slamming her fork onto the table. "I'm sorry. Let's not talk about this right now. It's your birthday."

Sensing the unsettling nature of the conversation, Aurora decided not to persist with her questioning. "I think I may have found the sequence for glioblastoma."

"Oh, that's fantastic, Aurora. I always knew you would make us proud with your discoveries," Jasmine replied as she tidied the dinner plates from the table.

Aurora gave a half-baked smile.

"I thought you would be happy about that?" asked Jasmine.

Aurora looked out through the metallic-pane windows. "I am. It's just—"

"Just what?"

"Never mind."

Jasmine brought out a gigantic tiramisu cheesecake and placed it on the table.

Jasmine rounded up Barry, after a great deal of persistence and they sang the Cooinda Birthday song. It was a traditional song composed by Apollo, a well-regarded pop star.

"Make a wish," smiled Jasmine.

Aurora closed her eyes and made a wish. Almost at the same time, she felt her ACCESS vibrate. She opened her eyes and looked at her wrist. *'You are feeling optimistic.'*

Barry took a slice of cake and disappeared from the table. Jasmine left the room momentarily, returning with her hands behind her back. "Twenty-one years ago, you entered this world. You have grown into a beautiful, intelligent, caring, and curious woman. We are all proud of you, Aurora." Jasmine handed Aurora her gift. "Happy Birthday, sweetheart."

Aurora carefully removed the blue polymer wrapping, revealing a necklace with a locket. Inside the locket was a beautifully framed bluish-green flower. "Oh, mum. Thank you," exclaimed Aurora, embracing her mother.

"Do you like it?" asked Jasmine.

"Of course," replied Aurora. "What is it though?"

"It's the flower of Cooinda. It's from the Red Cedar tree."

Aurora couldn't keep her eyes off the flower. "It's so pretty," she said finally, fastening the necklace around her neck. She smiled at her mother. "I think I might go to bed. Thank you for dinner and the gift. They are beautiful."

Jasmine once again embraced her daughter and gave her a peck on the cheek.

"Happy Birthday, sweetheart."

Aurora made her way upstairs and collapsed onto her bed, looking out over the roofs of Cooinda. The starless sky was intensely dark. The only light visible was that produced by the Source, along with the streetlights that were powered by it. At this time of the day, the Source gave out a blue hue allowing for Cooinda's inhabitants to relax.

She could still not shift her thoughts about her dream earlier. She held onto her necklace and eventually drifted off to sleep.

Chapter 2

The twenty-year-old 4WD vibrated intensely, maxed out at eighty kilometres an hour while travelling along the Landsborough Highway towards Winton.

Oliver Ritchie and Tom Hobson were best friends throughout high school and university. They were on their final leg of a grand tour of the outback, collecting data and geological specimens. Oliver had just completed his university degree in geology, majoring in palaeontology. His fascination with fossils, particularly dinosaurs, began at an early age. By the age of five, he was already able to name and categorise almost one hundred species of dinosaurs. His particular interest was the *Australovenator wintonensis*. It was the only species of its type to be found in this part of the country. It measured over two meters tall and up to six meters long. Its main survival advantage was its speed. It was postulated that it was able to reach cheetah-like speeds chasing down an appetising meal.

Tom studied geology too but spent more time at the university recreation hall flirting with the women.

"It's hard to believe that this entire area was flooded with water one-hundred and ten million years ago," said Oliver, exuberantly.

Tom scanned the red dirt landscape. "Here?"

"Yeah, this is a huge basin."

"Yeah, right. You've got it up here," said Tom pointing to his head. "I've got it down there," he said pointing to his lap.

Oliver shook his head and smiled. "Good thing I still enjoy your company all the same. Despite your practical jokes."

"You remember our last day at St Simon's?"

"How could I forget?" laughed Oliver.

It had always been a tradition to carry out some form of retribution to any number of teachers as a parting gift, and Tom was more than ready to continue the tradition.

Mitch, another friend of both Tom and Oliver, acted as a decoy. He distracted Mr Scott, the physics teacher, by having him go over some complex circular momentum workings on the whiteboard. Tom swiped Mr Scott's car keys from off the desk and settled them into his trouser pocket. There was one more class period after physics class, and Tom was set with this plan.

The bell sounded and Tom walked with purpose towards the staff car park. Pressing the remote repeatedly as he walked down the rows of cars, he finally located Mr Scott's vehicle. The number plate read TOPTEACH. The car was immaculate from the exterior. It was obvious Mr Scott admired his Porsche Taycanin. Tom pondered for a minute as to how his esteemed teacher was able to afford such an appreciable-looking vehicle and half contemplated whether he should abandon his plan. He had gone too far, though, to give up now. Besides, there was a tradition to be upheld.

Tom opened the driver seat door and settled into the beige-leathered bucket seats. He felt at home and could envision himself driving around in this prize of a car out of the grounds and onto the main road. His plan wasn't to start the vehicle. It was to inject the air-conditioning vents with confetti and fill the car with inflated balloons.

Half an hour passed, and Tom had finally squeezed in the last of the balloons into the car. He gently closed the door and made his way back towards the school, returned the keys onto Mr Scott's desk, and waited for the final bell to sound.

High School was done forever, and Oliver, Mitch, and Tom gave each other a shove and a fist bump and escaped the grounds before Mr Scott realised his present.

Oliver's parents were not overly keen on Tom and were concerned that his influences might rub off on Oliver's impeccable academic record.

"So how did you break the news to your folks that you were road-tripping with their favourite bad influence?" asked Tom.

"I make my own decisions," replied Oliver.

"Yeah, right," snickered Tom.

A siren sounded. Oliver looked in the rear vision mirror and saw a police car flashing its lights. "What's going on here?" He indicated and slowed the 4WD to a stop off the road. A policeman stepped out of his vehicle and approached the 4WD, guarding his holstered gun.

"G'day boys. I'm Constable Rob Carlson. How are we today?" asked the policeman through the open window.

"Hi there officer," replied Tom, grinning around Oliver. "Anything wrong?"

"Well that depends, doesn't it," replied the officer. "Drivers licence please."

Oliver ferreted through the centre console to locate his wallet and his identification. "Have we done anything wrong, officer?" he asked, nervously handing over his licence to the officer.

"Not yet," smiled the officer. "Just doing a random check, that's all."

Oliver looked around the deserted highway. "Ok."

The officer entered the details of Oliver's licence into his hand-held computer before asking, "What brings you boys out this way, anyway?"

"Looking for a bit of trouble, if you know what I mean," winked Tom.

The officer looked up from his computer screen. "No, I don't know what you mean. Have you had anything to drink in the previous twenty-four hours?"

Oliver shook his head.

The officer pulled a breathalyser from his pocket and held it in front of Oliver's mouth. "Please state your name," he instructed.

"Oliver Ritchie."

"Thank you," replied the officer. "Ok, that seems to be in order. Have you used drugs recently?"

Oliver shook his head.

"What about you, sir?" asked the officer to Tom.

Tom looked at Oliver with apologetic looking eyes.

"Tom!" exclaimed Oliver.

"What have you had?" asked the officer.

"Nothing really."

"What's nothing really?"

"I may have had a joint or two last night," replied Tom looking down towards his feet.

The officer produced a swab and handed it to Oliver. "Please swab your tongue and cheeks for me, please."

Oliver did as he was told and handed the swab back to the officer.

The officer placed the swab into a canister and connected it to an electronic reader. "The DrugScan did not detect any drugs in your system," he declared.

Oliver sighed with relief.

"Are you the sole driver of this vehicle?" asked the officer, not taking his eyes off Tom.

"Yes, sir," replied Oliver.

The police officer handed back Oliver's licence and inspected the 4WD, tapping each wheel as he went. "Do you two mind stepping out of the vehicle," he instructed when he arrived at the rear of the 4WD.

Both Oliver and Tom got out of the vehicle and presented to the officer.

"Can you please open the boot?" asked the officer.

Oliver opened the boot. His face went pale.

"Care to explain this?" asked the officer.

Oliver looked at Tom with consternation.

"What?" replied Tom. "It's not what you think."

The officer picked up a steak knife with his gloved hands. "What's this, then?"

"I can explain," said Tom.

The officer next picked up a pair of gloves and a headlamp. "And this?"

"I have an issue with cleanliness. It's when I need to go—" said Tom.

"Go?"

"You know? Number two. I prefer gloves so I don't have to wash my hands."

"Hmm."

"What about this?" asked the officer picking up duct tape.

"That's for this crappy 4WD," smiled Tom.

"Hey!" exclaimed Oliver.

The officer looked at Oliver with suspicion.

"What do we have here?" said the officer picking up a large garbage bag. He opened the bag and threw its contents onto the ground. "Bones."

"Yeah, they're Ollie's," said Tom, pointing at Oliver. "He got those. 'They're his favourite'," he said.

The officer looked both Tom and Oliver up and down. "You two have some explaining to do."

"Look, I know this probably looks a bit sus," said Oliver, his eyes focused on the scattered bones."

"A bit?" replied the officer, looking over his RayBan sunglasses.

"We're on a road trip to check out fossils. These are some old bones we bought from a local out here. The tape is to hold the Beast together," continued Oliver.

"The Beast?" the officer inquired.

"Yeah, that's what he calls this piece of—" added Tom.

"And the knife?" the officer, interjected.

Oliver looked at Tom and shrugged.

"Everyone needs a knife out here!" exclaimed Tom.

"Do they?" replied the officer, stroking his chin. "I can't charge you two with anything, but I have to say you two are a little odd. Especially you," he said, pointing at Tom. "Go on. Get out of here, before I find something."

Oliver and Tom settled back into their 4WD and continued their adventure. Oliver checked the rear vision mirror every few kilometres, just to be sure the officer hadn't changed his mind.

"Bloody hell. That was a bit hectic," said Tom after a long silence.

"Gloves? Really?" replied Oliver.

The 4WD slowed as it entered the sleepy town of Winton and they came to a stop at their resting place for the night, the Winton Outback Motel.

"Well, here we are," said Oliver.

They collected their overnight bags from the back seat and made their way towards the hotel.

"How's ya going?" asked the receptionist. The badge said BRUCE.

"Good. We're wondering if you have any rooms available?" asked Oliver.

"Let's see now." Bruce cleared his throat and sifted through the placard of keys. Every single hook was occupied. "Looks like you might be in luck," replied Bruce, placing a key on the desk. "It's been crazy, busy lately."

"How much a night?" asked Oliver.

"One-fifty," replied Bruce.

"One-fifty!" exclaimed Tom. "That's—"

"That'll be fine," Oliver interrupted.

"Not a problem," smiled Bruce. "Oh, do you need a wake-up call?"

"No, it should be right," replied Oliver.

"What brings you into town?" asked Bruce.

"Ollie likes rocks and dinosaurs," grinned Tom.

"Do you?" said Bruce, leaning his hairy arm on the desk. "My suggestion is to check out the Trackways. Get there early though, hey. Bloody crowds of tourists will be swarming the area by noon."

"Thanks, Bruce," said Oliver.

"Pleasure. If there's anything else I can help you boys with just give me a holler."

"Will do," replied Tom.

The lads collected their key and walked down the corridor towards their room.

"He's a bit of a strange one, ain't he?" Tom said.

"Who?"

Tom nodded his head towards the front desk. "Bruce."

Oliver chuckled. "Yeah, they're a bit different out here mate. You'd fit right in here, I reckon."

"Piss off! At least I ain't all stuck up," Tom said with a smile.

They found their room. It wasn't a fancy six-star room by any means, but it had all the necessities including wireless Internet, a stocked-up bar fridge, and two firm single beds, as requested.

"Well, we better get some rest, Tom," said Oliver, inspecting the mattress.

"Bloody hell! These beds are like concrete" replied Tom, thumping his fist into the bed. "I've slept on some pretty hard surfaces, but this here takes the cake."

Oliver laughed.

"Night Tom."

"Night, mate."

* * *

The next morning, upon hearing the alarm clock, Tom cried out in agony. "Fuck! My back. That had to be the worst fucking bed I have ever slept on."

Oliver sat up in bed. "Where the hell is the alarm clock?"

"It's in the top drawer," replied Tom, massaging his sore back.

Oliver opened the drawer, of the bedside table, and received a face full of flour. "Ah, shit!"

Tom was in hysterics.

"Bloody hell, Tom!" exclaimed Oliver, blowing flour rings.

Tom would chuckle every time he looked at Oliver's face. "So what time is it, Ollie?"

Oliver gave up on the alarm clock, concerned that if he were to open any other drawers, they, too, might deliver an unwelcome gift. Instead, he found his mobile phone. 8:10 am.

"Bloody hell. The morning is almost half over," said Oliver, leaping out of bed and changing into his day clothes, not even bothering to shower.

"Righto, so where are we off to first?" asked Tom.

"I thought we might check out the musical fence."

"Musical fence? What the hell is that?"

"You'll see."

Oliver and Tom packed their belongings and checked out of the hotel.

"How was your sleep, boys?" inquired Bruce.

"Mate, you gotta do something about those beds, hey?" replied Tom. "My back is killing me."

Bruce looked at Tom and said, "We have a day spa if you want to use that?"

Tom wasn't sure if he was serious or not, and his facial expression gave nothing away. "Nah, it's cool. It should sort itself out soon."

Bruce finally cracked a smile. "Alright. Thanks for dropping by and enjoy your trip, lads." Bruce turned away to restock the key holder.

The boys got into their LandCruiser and started it up, but not without a great deal of noise and fumes.

"Shitty car," said Tom.

"Hey," replied Oliver, patting the dash. "The Beast has been good to me. It's done more mileage than Apollo 11, I reckon. And it's still going."

"Only just," replied Tom. "Righto, let's find this fence and get on with this day so that we can see the town and its ladies."

The 4WD exited the motel's car park and they made their way to the first stop. The musical fence.

Chapter 3

The Source projected a heliotrope purple over the city. The night shifted towards morning.

"Alright, another day," Aurora muttered to herself. She might have only turned twenty-one yesterday, but she felt a great deal older. It was the monotony of her life. At the laboratory, she worked fifteen-hour days, oftentimes, six days a week. The time spent working on her scientific endeavours meant she missed a great deal else. She had recently overheard Eliza, another research scientist, in the lunchroom gushing over Jake.

"Jake was so brave," said Eliza.

"What happened?" asked one of her friends.

"The Trophtec Trojans were annihilating the Syndbio Saints. Jake had just scored this awesome goal and looked over to us."

"You mean you?"

Eliza giggled. "Naturally. Anyway whilst he was looking at me, this massive guy from the other team collected him."

"Oh, no. Was he alright?"

"There was blood everywhere."

"What did you do?"

"I took care of him, of course. I ran to the first aid kit and grabbed some sealant."

"You are so right for him, Eliza."

"I know. He owes me one."

Aurora had wished she hadn't overheard the conversation. She wished that it had been her nursing Jake back to good health.

She made her way to the shower and dressed in her usual attire. Grey slacks and a short-sleeved grey top. *I wish my wardrobe had some colour.*

There wasn't enough time for breakfast. Aurora had slept in, which was unusual for her. She left the house and jogged towards the monorail station. Her ACCESS sounded all sorts of alarms. Low sugar, excessive heart rate, lack of sleep.

Aurora entered the Trophtec laboratory and stood at the gate. *Open the gate,* she thought. Upon confirmation of her identity, the gates opened, and she entered the main atrium. There were several paths she could take depending upon the area of interest. Down the orange path to the left was the robotics department. The centre path, the blue trail, led to the artificial intelligence department. The green path on the right was the path that Aurora followed; the molecular biology and disease restoration section.

People zipped around the building like ants in a functioning nest. Jake had already arrived and was setting up various assays. "Morning Aurora."

"Morning."

"How was your birthday celebration?"

"Yeah, it was ok, thanks. Nothing special, just another birthday." Aurora placed her bag onto the bench and retrieved her lab coat.

"How are you getting on with your experiments?" asked Jake.

"Yeah, they're fine," responded Aurora.

"Everything alright?"

"Yeah, why wouldn't it be?" Aurora twirled her finger in her hair and pretended to be preoccupied with switching on her microscope. It was true; she lacked focus. Since that dream, Aurora was unsettled.

"Hey, Jake, have you ever wondered what is outside these walls?" she asked.

"Ah, sure. Did you want me to show you around Cooinda?" he asked hopefully.

"No. I mean, outside of Cooinda?" pressed Aurora.

Jake contemplated before shrugging. "Don't know. Never really given that much thought, to be honest," replied Jake. "Besides, where else would you rather be? Cooinda is the best. Look at the scientific work our city does. We have pretty much non-existent crime, we work when we want to work, and we have so much freedom to do whatever we want."

Aurora nodded. "Perhaps you're right. Maybe I should be content with what I have," replied Aurora, clutching her necklace. Internally, Aurora was frustrated. She couldn't understand why she felt she was the only one questioning her place in Cooinda. What's more, she was sceptical of how much freedom the people of Cooinda did have.

"Oh, cool necklace. Was that a gift for your birthday?" asked Jake.

"Yeah, from my mum," replied Aurora.

Jake got off his chair to inspect the locket. "What's inside?"

Aurora sensed Jake staring at her breasts, which made her feel uncomfortable. Wanting to distract his attention she opened the locket to reveal the flower. "Apparently it's Cooinda's flower. Some cedar tree or something."

"Wow, it's pretty. It suits you."

Aurora blushed. "Thanks." She tucked the chain into her top and looked around the laboratory to determine her first task of the day.

"Morning!" called Eliza.

"Oh, hi Eliza," replied Jake, looking up from his bench.

"So, when are you taking me out to dinner, Jake?" asked Eliza, batting her eyelashes through her cylindrical-lens glasses. She flicked her hair and surreptitiously touched Jake's arm.

Aurora glanced towards Jake who moved away from Eliza, pretending to continue with his work.

"Ah, I don't know. I'm pretty busy at the moment."

Aurora interjected, "Weren't you just telling me how much freedom you enjoy in Cooinda, Jake?"

Jake gave Aurora a death stare. "Thanks, Aurora. I'll get back to you Eliza."

"Oh, ok, yeah, sure," replied Eliza, turning towards the exit, giving Aurora's chair a deliberate shove on the way.

"What is with that girl?" Aurora's ACCESS vibrated. *You are feeling a hint of jealousy.*

Jake didn't respond. The duo continued working for the next few hours before Jake momentarily left the lab. Aurora went to her digital table and logged into the Cooinda Intranet. It was a useful display of the recent advances in Cooinda, newsworthy items, and interviews with its citizens. There were no social media. Aurora typed in the phrase, *Life outside of Cooinda* into the search browser. The computer churned for a second before displaying, *No results were found.* She then typed in, *Cooinda Cedar.* Aurora nervously looked behind her to see if Jake had returned. *The Cooinda Cedar is a fast-growing evergreen tree that grows to heights of 35 metres. Like all the plants in Cooinda, the Cedar tree grows hydroponically, utilising salt-enriched water contained in an underground basin.*

"Hey, isn't that the same flower that you have in your necklace?" Jake asked.

Aurora almost leapt out of her chair in fright. "Far out, Jake! You scared me."

Jake chuckled. "Sorry about that. I didn't mean to scare you. Why are you looking at that anyway? You know that we're only supposed to use the computers for work purposes, right?"

Aurora was annoyed that everyone in Cooinda was so rule-bound. She closed the screen and resumed her work.

"Besides, if you want to know anything, just ask the Divine."

"True. Come to think of it, my Divine Day is in a few days."

"Given you practically live at this place you should have accumulated a heap of time to ask a heap of questions," smiled Jake.

Aurora giggled. "I bet you didn't know that McPherson's once made bubble gum flavoured broccoli?"

"McPherson's? The fast-food joint? I didn't know that. Maybe I should work more too so I can find out just as useless, trivial information."

"Oh, and did you know that the taste of cheese changes depending on what music you listen to?"

"I don't need to go to the Divine now," chuckled Jake. "I can rely on your knowledge. Ok, I did learn something."

"You did?"

Jake nodded. "I overheard in the corridor the other day, a researcher here, named Zeno—"

"Is that his first name or last?"

"Not sure, everyone just calls him Zeno. Anyway, these researchers reckon he's been able to alter how quickly or slowly change of something can occur."

"How?"

"By measuring it. Apparently, if you observe or measure something more frequently, the decaying process of death slows."

"Would you really want to live forever, though?"

"Absolutely," replied Jake, flexing his biceps.

"Oh, hey, I'm going to pick up my first car today," Jake said, visibly excited.

"Oh, that's cool," replied Aurora.

"Why don't you go and request your car?"

"I prefer the monorails. Besides, I don't go out much anyway. What brand is the car you're getting?"

"It's the new Magnetra."

"Is that the one that hovers higher than the others on the road?" Aurora asked, remembering what she'd seen her father watch on the TV last night.

"Only a bit higher, but its AI is much smarter than the others. It detects collisions from further back so you don't spill your coffee if it has to brake," Jake boasted. "Do you maybe want to go for a ride with me tomorrow?"

"Ah, no thanks. I have a few things to do."

"Ok, ah, maybe another time then," Jarrod replied despondently.

"Sure." She didn't need to look at her ACCESS to know how she was feeling at this point. She felt vexed that she hadn't enjoyed the freedoms that her colleagues had, though also felt guilt in not heeding her mother's words of wisdom. After all, her mother, like most mothers, had been a teacher, a carer, a nurse, everything. She admired her mother and respected her.

Chapter 4

Tom thrashed the wired fence with his drumsticks, producing a deafening sound of chimes and gongs that resonated off the tin shelter.

"Come on, Ollie. We better get going. Remember what Bruce said about getting to the quarry before noon?"

"Oh, do we have to leave?" Tom moved to the drum kit, made of rusted car parts.

"You're a big kid. You can do more banging, later on, mate."

Tom gave the rusty bucket drum kit one last smack before hopping into the LandCruiser, with Oliver.

"Bloody hell these seats are uncomfortable. It's like sitting on a cactus. So what's at this quarry, anyway?"

"Are you serious? There's a giant dinosaur monument and foot impressions," replied Oliver, starting the engine.

"Sounds like a hoot. Then we can hit the town?"

"No, then we head to the Waltzing Matilda Centre."

"What? We're not leaving much time for actual fun," said Tom, pulling his Akubra hat over his face.

"There will be. Later tonight. I promise."

"Maybe I'll find a girl for you, mate."

Oliver had gone on a few dates with girls from his university class, but none of them had gone well.

On one particular date, he'd taken an attractive young woman named Melissa to an Italian restaurant. It was a quaint little restaurant fitted out with all things Italian, including the giant pepper grinder and the quintessential Italian flag draped like a canopy over the tables. The date was going well in Oliver's mind, at least.

"So should we have a starter?" Oliver asked, attempting to make small talk.

"No, I'd rather make room for dessert," remarked Melissa.

Not dissuaded, Oliver went back to reviewing the menu.

Being a Wednesday night there were only three other couples, so the waitress was soon aside the table ready to take their orders.

"I'll have the mushroom risotto, please," said Oliver, not looking up from his menu.

"And I will go the fettuccine rose," said Melissa, pointing where the item was on the menu.

"Certainly," replied the waitress as she whisked away.

The scent of perfume from the waitress lingered in the air. Melissa grabbed hold of her glass of water before asking, "So, tell me, if you passed a mobile speed camera whilst travelling along a road, would you flash your headlights to oncoming traffic to alert them?"

Oliver's eyes widened, and he could instantly feel beads of sweat forming on the back of his neck. He adjusted his shirt collar to breathe a little easier. Clearing his throat he stammered, "Ah, I don't know. I think I would, yes."

Melissa took a swig of water, before firmly placing her emptied glass onto the table.

"So you're ok with people breaking the law?"

Oliver could feel his carotid pulsating in his neck.

"No! I mean, I guess. I'm just helping them not get a fine."

"So they should get away with speeding?"

"I, I don't know," replied Oliver, looking towards the kitchen.

"How can you not know?"

"I don't feel strongly about it."

"You felt strongly enough to flash your headlights."

"This is stupid."

Melissa gently placed her napkin onto the table, pushed back her chair, stood up and cancelled her order with the waitress. Oliver sat perplexed. However, he decided to stay seated and enjoy his mushroom risotto.

Oliver crunched the gears up to third. It was as far as it went. The engine shrieked as though in pain. Oliver didn't know how much longer the 4WD would last but hoped it would at least get them back home to Brisbane.

"Surely your rich parents could have bought you something decent, mate," said Tom, attempting to fasten his frayed seatbelt.

"I left home straight after school, remember?" replied Oliver. "All my parents care about is their reputations. I don't want to be pretentious as them." Oliver's eyes glistened. "You have no idea what it's like to live in a family that are so full of themselves. Do you think it's all champagne and roses? Trust me, it's not."

"Settle down, mate. I was only having your leg," replied Tom.

The drive to the footprint was eerily quiet. Once they arrived at the site, Oliver's enthusiasm returned.

"Right, let's check out this foot, hey?" Oliver raced past a tour guide with her small group of people to inspect the ground, pitted with thousands of impressions. "Tom! Would you have a look at this?"

"Coming," replied Tom, kicking his shoes through the red

dirt.

"So, what we have here are prints from a theropod dinosaur, as well as hundreds of ornithopods. Probably attempting to escape being eaten by the giant meat-eater," announced the tour guide.

"A stampede! Cool!" exclaimed Tom. "You could make a movie about that."

Oliver looked towards Tom, shaking his head.

"What?"

The sun was fierce, and many within the tour group fanned themselves.

"Bloody hell, it's getting warm, ain't it?" said Tom.

"Sure is," replied Oliver, taking the last remaining skerricks of water from his water bottle. "What say we go check out the Waltzing Matilda? Surely that would be air-conditioned."

"Sounds good to me," replied Tom.

They travelled an hour and a half back towards town and located the museum. Tom ran over to the bronzed statue out front of the museum.

"Hey, Ollie! Take a photo. This guy is almost as good looking as me, don't you reckon?"

Oliver took his phone from his pocket and captured Tom alongside Banjo Patterson.

"What sort of name is that, anyway?" said Tom, reading the plaque.

"He's only one of the most famous Aussie poets, mate," replied Oliver. "He wrote the poem, Waltzing Matilda"

"Waltzing Matilda is a poem? I always thought that she was that giant kangaroo, I saw on TV, that winked its way around the track at the Commonwealth Games."

"I think you might need to brush up on your Australian

history," replied Oliver.

"Mate. I'm all historied out. When are we going to check out the nightlife?"

It was already three o'clock in the afternoon. It was clear that Tom's tolerance had well and truly waned. "Come on, Ollie, I think we're done now, mate," said Oliver, unimpressed that he hadn't properly inspected the museum.

Tom's face lit up. He raced around to the passenger seat and stuck his head out the window, like a dog going on an outing to the beach.

Chapter 5

Aurora mixed various restriction enzymes into her DNA samples. She stared absently at her row of Eppendorf tubes and reflected on why she had chosen to be a scientist. Her father's ill health had been a strong driving force. Aurora's eyes welled upon thinking of her father's anguish.

"Dad, are you ok?" Aurora asked her father, as he collapsed onto the floor clutching onto the kitchen table. Aurora could see the frightened look on his face. He was gasping for air.

"Aurora, get mum," he whimpered.

"Mum!" yelled Aurora.

Jasmine ran into the kitchen and saw Barry quivering on the floor. He was turning blue.

"Aurora, call an ambulance," instructed Jasmine.

Aurora flicked through her address book on her wrist device.

"Cooinda Emergency, how may I assist?" the operator answered.

"It's my father, he's having trouble breathing," said Aurora frantically.

The paramedics arrived at the house within a few minutes and took Barry to the Cooinda hospital. He was pumped with a cocktail of drugs to keep him alive.

"He's very lucky, you know?" said one of the treating doctors.

"What's wrong with him?" asked Aurora.

The doctor took both Aurora's and Jasmine's hands. "We don't know, but we are running more tests. As soon as we know, you'll know."

Aurora was terrified. After two weeks in hospital, Barry received his diagnosis. Granulomatosis with polyangiitis. He was released from the hospital and sent home, where he slowly recovered. The medication suppressed his immune system. It was a good thing that Cooinda didn't have any infectious diseases. Aurora despised the suffering her father went through and she made it her mission to remedy this through her scientific work.

She looked around the bench in a frenzy. "Jake, have you seen where I put my DNA polymerase?"

Jake joined Aurora in looking around the spotless laboratory. Everything was neatly labelled and not a piece of equipment was left lying around for too long.

"Ah, here it is," Jake quipped, opening his hand.

Aurora was annoyed that she was distracted. "Thanks," she replied as she took the vial from Jake's hand.

"So, are you going to the Source Festival this weekend?" asked Jake

There was a solid ten-second delay before she processed what Jake had just said. "Ah, I don't think so."

"Oh, come on. It'll be fun," he grinned.

"I don't know. What is the festival?"

"Are you serious? Do you seriously not know what the Source Festival is?"

"I seriously don't know what the Source Festival is."

Jake's expression of dismay said it all. "They have music and dancing, all in honour of the Source, of course."

"I don't get it. Why do people get so focused on a light source? It's almost as though they worship the thing."

"You should be thankful for the Source, Aurora. It provides us with warmth, light, and energy."

Aurora rolled her eyes.

"Look, come with me, and I promise you, you won't regret it," Jake said gently.

Aurora contemplated while Jake continued staring at her. Having never experienced life outside of work and home, Aurora was curious about what the festival was. She felt it was time to live her life. She hoped her mother would understand. "Fine," she groaned. "I'll go, but you have to promise me that I can leave at any time."

"Absolutely," Jake said excitedly. He smiled like a Cheshire cat.

The two of them worked solidly in silence for a few hours before Hayden Morrisey, who worked in the AI department, walked in and yelled, "Hey, you guys! You coming to lunch?"

Both Jake and Aurora were startled by Hayden's entrance.

"How did you get in here?" snarled Aurora.

"I have my means," smiled Hayden. "Come on. You two are all work and no play."

"We'll be there in a sec," said Jake, looking at his ACCESS.

Hayden pressed the button on the centrifuge and watched it spin, hypnotised by its motion.

"Hayden! Are you right?" Aurora said, agitated by his childish behaviour.

Hayden pressed the button again and the rotors slowed. "Sorry."

"You ready, then?" said Jake to Aurora.

"I guess," replied Aurora, returning her pipette onto its

holder.

The lunchroom was spacious. Five hundred employees worked at Trophtec at any one time, although Jake and Aurora's department was distinctly smaller.

"So, what have you guys been up to?" Hayden asked while opening his lunchbox.

Aurora quietly assessed Hayden. Aurora held little regard for him. She found him immature, despite his age of nearly thirty.

"Aurora and I are going to the Source Festival," Jake announced with delight.

"Oh, awesome! Can I come too?" asked Hayden.

Jake looked over to Aurora, who pretended to admire the manicured garden out the window. She was annoyed with Hayden's lack of social etiquette.

"Well, Aurora and I were—," Jake replied.

"Excellent," said Hayden.

The nerve of the guy thought Aurora.

"Can you believe that festival has been running for ten years?" Hayden mumbled in between bites of his frittata.

Aurora studied Hayden intently. *Ten years? Why have I never heard of it?* "Has it been advertised?" she asked.

Hayden finished devouring his meal and licked his fingers for completeness. "Has what been advertised?"

"The Source Festival or whatever it is called?" said Aurora, clenching her hands in frustration.

"Oh, I don't know. It's kind of a known thing," replied Hayden, looking into Aurora's lunchbox. "You eating any of that?"

Aurora looked at her uneaten vegetable wrap and pushed her lunchbox aside.

"You not feeling well, Aurora?" asked Jake.

"I've kind of lost my appetite," replied Aurora, staring at Hayden.

"Maybe it's the phantom element," snickered Hayden.

Aurora's attention immediately shifted to Hayden. "Huh? The what?"

Hayden's eyes were fixated on Aurora's lunch. "The phantom element."

Jake grunted. "Oh, not this again," said Jake, sitting back in his chair.

"What? You must admit it sounds plausible," said Hayden. "You sure you aren't eating that?"

Aurora shoved her lunchbox to Hayden, who rummaged through it like a hyena eating a leftover carcass.

"I think it's ridiculous, that's what I think," added Jake.

Aurora watched the conversation between Jake and Hayden. "Would someone tell me what is going on here?" exclaimed Aurora, who brought the entire room to silence.

"Would someone tell me what is going on here," she repeated, this time in a whisper.

Hayden took a huge bite of Aurora's food. "This wrap is delicious, Aurora."

Jake started, "Hayden once told me about this stupid theory—"

"Stupid? It's not stupid," said Hayden, still chewing his food.

"The story goes that this element—"

"Phantom element," Hayden interjected again, wiping the tomato seeds from his mouth.

"Thank you, Hayden," continued Jake. "Thousands of people—"

"Millions," Hayden corrected.

"Did you want to tell the story?" said Jake to Hayden.

"No, no, you're telling it so well," grinned Hayden.

"Millions of people got sick. Many of them died," Jake added.

Aurora gasped. "What? It kills people? Is it like cancer?"

Jake shrugged and looked at Hayden for elaboration. "Hayden?"

"Huh? Oh, yeah, I don't know. I think it's some sort of invisible force that makes people sick."

Aurora winced.

"That's why we're all here," Hayden continued.

"All here? What do you mean?" replied Aurora, drawing her chair closer to the table.

"Apparently McPherson built this city for us. To protect us from the phantom element," said Hayden.

"I don't understand," frowned Aurora.

"What else is there to explain?" replied Hayden, folding his arms across his chest.

"Let me see if I have this correct," Aurora continued. "There's a mysterious, invisible force, which you call the phantom element, that somehow causes disease, and people die from it?"

"Yep."

"And McPherson then built this city to protect us from it?"

"Yes."

"See why I think it's preposterous?" replied Jake.

Aurora was frustrated in not being able to properly comprehend Hayden's theory. *On one hand, it made sense, yet there were many more questions to be had.*

"Why is this the first time I've heard about this?" asked Aurora.

Hayden shrugged. "I don't know. Maybe you just haven't

talked to the right people."

"The right people?" said Aurora, perplexed.

"Who told you this stupid theory anyway?" asked Jake.

"My dad."

"What makes you think he knows all this?" said Aurora, annoyed with Hayden's cockiness.

Hayden shrugged. "I don't know, but he did show me this awesome-looking scar on his arm. He said it was from some sort of medicine they injected into him to protect him from the phantom element. Anyway, what time should we get to the festival?" said Hayden, changing the subject.

"Whose we?" Aurora asked, folding her arms.

"Oh, Crystal," replied Hayden.

Jake threw up his arms. "Sure, why not. The more the merrier."

"Cool. So around six?" Hayden asked.

Aurora momentarily closed her eyes and counted to ten to calm her nerves.

"Sure," replied Jake.

Hayden focused his attention on his wrist device and immediately stood up. "Hey, you guys, I have to go. I'm running a new neural networking program; it's very exciting." And with that, Hayden hurried out of the room, leaving Jake and Aurora alone.

"Well, I guess we better get back to work," said Jake, closing the lid on his lunchbox.

"What the?"

"What?"

"You're not at all concerned about the phantom element? What if he's right? What if we all escaped?"

"Unlikely, Aurora. Don't you think we'd remember it?"

Aurora pondered for a bit. "Maybe."

"As I said, it's a conspiracy story. It's like that song, Ripping, by Apollo."

"What about it?"

"You know? If you play it backward it tells you the date when Cooinda will end."

Aurora shook her head. "I haven't heard of that one either." Despite the temperature not ever-changing in Cooinda, she got goosebumps.

"So what time should I pick you up tomorrow?" asked Jake.

Aurora stood up with a renewed lease of life in anticipation of exploring beyond her home. "Make it five. You can come around for an early dinner."

"Cool, What's your address?"

Aurora typed her address into her wrist device and pressed *SEND* to Jake.

BEEP!

"Oh! Someone has sent me a message," said Jake, looking at his wrist.

Aurora rolled her eyes.

Chapter 6

Oliver awoke to the sounds of squawking ibis. "God! How much did we drink last night?"

Tom rolled over, the sun in his eyes. "How the hell did we end up here?"

Oliver looked around the abandoned recreational park. The only activity was a rusty swing that squealed in the breeze.

"You look like you had a good time last night, Tom?"

"Oh yeah, buddy. It was great. Feeling a bit worse for wear this morning, though. Hey, how hot was Emma? I can't believe how strong her legs were."

Oliver contemplated whether to tell his good mate that his lady friend was, in fact, a transvestite. *Nah, better not*, Oliver thought to himself.

"Right, so where are we off today, Ollie?" asked Tom taking a sip of his stale, warm beer, still by his side.

"I'm thinking we head to Quilpie to check out some Boulder opal."

"Great, more fossils. Do you think there will be just as hot chicks in Quilpie as there is here?"

Oliver hesitated. "Possibly."

The boys grabbed their overnight bags and threw them in the back of the LandCruiser.

Oliver turned the engine over and it heard it hiss. "Ugh, looks like the Beast is thirsty again."

"This damn, piece of shit of a vehicle is sucking us dry," said Tom, stretching out his body.

Oliver poured his bottle of water into the radiator. "She's happy now by the looks of it."

"That makes one of us."

Oliver closed the bonnet and started the engine and they made their way out of the town.

Tom extended his legs onto the dashboard and relaxed into his seat for the long journey. "Not much out here, is there?" he said, scanning the bare landscape.

"Nope," replied Oliver.

"Hey! I'm thinking of starting a business."

"Oh yeah? What sort of business?"

"I'm thinking like an outback tour. I'll hire a bus, pick up people from the big smoke, and show them the sights and sounds of the outback. There will be a pub crawl after each night. What ya think?"

Oliver's right eye twitched. "Maybe, mate."

Tom fanned out his hands as though presenting to a group of venture capitalists. "I can see it now!" exclaimed Tom.

"You're a go-getter, mate. I give you that." laughed Oliver. "But then, you've always been one not to shy away from things, hey?"

"I had to mate. Us Simmons had to stick together." Tom inspected his tanned arms. "I hope that prick is rotting in hell."

"Who?"

"My fucked-up father."

"I had no idea mate," said Oliver, looking at Tom, who was gritting his teeth.

"Yeah, well, it was a long time ago."

"What about your mum?"

"What about her?"

"Was she?"

"We all were!" exclaimed Tom. "Me, mum, Alice, my sister."

"Jesus. I'm so sorry mate."

"Mum had to work three jobs just to support us. She was never home." Tom's eyes welled. "Then Alice found this dropkick who was only into her for the sex and in return got her high as a kite on drugs every day."

"Wow. You've certainly gone through a lot. My upbringing was a bloody fairy tale compared to yours by the sounds of it," said Oliver who threw a grin to Tom. He had never heard the story of Tom's troubled past. *Perhaps that's why he makes light of everything.*

Tom chuckled. "Yeah mate, you and your bloody prissy life."

"As I said, it wasn't all roses."

Tom pulled the sun visor down to shade his eyes. The warmth of the sun was putting him to sleep. His eyes began to get heavy before the 4WD jolted.

"What was that?"

Tom opened one eye and looked at Ollie. "What you do you mean, mate?"

Nothing.

CHUG! CHUG!

"There! You hear that?"

This time Tom had heard the sound, and it was increasing in frequency and intensity. The 4WD jerked, and the engine seized.

"Oh, God. We're going to die," screamed Tom.

The vehicle skidded from side to side taking out reflector

poles in the process. Oliver death-gripped the steering wheel.

"FARRRRK!" screamed Tom.

Tom dug his fingers into the upholstery, leaving behind permanent indentations. The Beast weaved from one side of the road to the other.

"Ollie! What are you doing?"

The air filled with smoke and the smell of burnt rubber. The vehicle spun a three-hundred-and-sixty-degree doughnut.

"We're going to die!" yelled Tom.

The Beast finally came to a stop in the dirt gutter. Both men were hyperventilating and sat motionless for a long while.

"You alright, Tom?" Oliver had sweat dripping off his forehead and his gelled hair had let go.

Tom exhaled heavily and patted his body. "Well, that woke me up."

Smoke emanated from under the hood. The two jumped out of the 4WD and moved away far enough in case it caught fire.

"Well, that's probably not good," remarked Tom.

Oliver rubbed his hands through his matted hair and inspected the surroundings. The land was flat and barren.

Oliver shakily pulled his mobile phone from his pocket. "No reception. Shit! What's yours say?"

Tom stood motionless, still in a state of shock.

"Tom!"

Tom shook his head. "Huh?"

"Your phone. Do you have reception?" implored Oliver, shaking Tom by the shoulders.

Tom pulled out his phone from his pocket and inspected the broken screen. "What the hell happened to my phone?"

"Alright, mate, I think we need to start walking and try to either hitch a ride or find someone to help us," said Oliver.

"Are you serious? We could die out here."

"Would you stop saying that? We're not going to die."

Oliver estimated it to be almost forty degrees Celsius, but the black bitumen reflecting the sun made it feel closer to fifty. They had only been walking for a few minutes, but their gait was already less coordinated and required more effort to stay upright.

"This heat is a killer," remarked Tom. "If we get stuck out here, I remember watching an episode of Bear Grylls where we dig a hole and piss into it, placing a plastic bag over the top, and within a few hours, it will be pure water."

Oliver glanced over at Tom, red-eyed from all the sweat that was burning his eyes. "I won't be drinking any of your pee, thanks, mate," he said with chagrin before glancing back over his shoulder. " How can there be absolutely no cars on this road? Unbelievable!"

An hour passed, and both had wished that the 4WD hadn't needed all their precious water. The plan was to refill their empty water bottles once they arrived at Quilpie.

Tom was heaving. Oliver, on the other hand, had remained active throughout his high school and university life and handled the heat a great deal better. He was an avid rower and earned a black belt in Taekwondo. His parents would have been proud of him.

"I'm not sure how much more I can take of this, mate," gasped Tom, holding his chest and wobbling from side to side as though having been subjected to a theme park ride for the last twenty minutes.

One of Tom's knees buckled and he collapsed onto the burning hot bitumen.

In the distance, Oliver could make out the outline of a house.

Or perhaps it was delirium.

"Look! Over there!" exclaimed Oliver, pointing in the direction of the house.

Tom was still trying to breathe but looked up and squinted. "What is it?"

"A house, you idiot. Do you not see it?"

Tom stood slowly while holding onto Oliver's waist and clawed himself up. "I can't see anything, mate," cried Tom.

Oliver took a few steps, dragging Tom behind. "You'll have to walk just a few more kilometres, I reckon. I can't carry you."

Tom let go of Oliver, dusting off his trousers. The dirt was incredibly red out here.

As they continued walking, it became obvious that Oliver wasn't hallucinating and could make out a giant corrugated iron roof atop a dilapidated white Colonial-style house. The door was missing from the front, along with much of the front veranda.

Nearing the fence, the two of them paused. "You reckon the fence is electrified, Ollie?"

Oliver extended his hand towards the fence. "Only one way to find out." He grabbed hold of the fence. "Ah!" cried Oliver, his hands wildly shaking the wire.

"What? What? What is it?" yelled Tom, backing away from Oliver, unsure of what to do.

Oliver burst into laughter, "You should have seen your face, mate."

"You bastard! I thought you were being fried!"

Oliver leaned forward with his hands on his knees, still in hysterics.

"Yeah, yeah, alright. I guess that's payback from all the pranks I've played on you."

Oliver crawled through the fence with Tom close behind while one of the Brangus cattle looked over in curiosity.

"I hope they're friendly," said Tom.

The house was maybe a few hundred metres away, a bit less if they were lucky.

"Great, more walking," declared Tom.

There was interest from more cattle as the two made their way up towards the house. Nearing the entrance, Oliver called out, "Hello! Anyone there?"

The air was incredibly still. So still that they could both hear the cattle treading on the dried grass some distance away.

"Hello!" Oliver cried again, in case the owners were preoccupied.

Standing atop the veranda, the floorboards creaked with every step.

"Hello! Anyone home?" Tom cried.

Oliver could hear his pulse. He estimated his heart was pumping over a hundred beats a minute. The sweat that had evaporated was replaced with fresh perspiration.

The house was dark from the outside. Perhaps it was abandoned.

"You go first," prompted Tom, giving Oliver's back a shove between the shoulder blades.

"Thanks, Tom," gasped Oliver.

Oliver continued into the darkened dwelling. It looked gigantic from the outside but within it was only a three-bedroom homestead.

"This must be the living room," exclaimed Oliver looking over towards a dusty LCD television set. "Tom?" Oliver could hear Tom telling a story to a herd of cattle. "Tom, what are you doing?"

Tom stopped his conversation and turned towards Oliver. "Hey, Ollie."

"Would you get in here?"

Tom moaned and stepped inside.

The hallway led them to the kitchen.

"How long has this place been here?" asked Tom.

"A while."

Tom turned the rusted taps and opened his mouth under the faucet waiting for water. "Come on. I'm so thirsty." Pipes could be heard rattling from underneath the floorboards. "Here it comes," he announced.

"I think it's blocked," said Oliver.

Tom turned the taps the other way. Still nothing.

A patter of little feet was heard at Tom's feet. He jumped into Oliver's already outstretched hands. "What the heck is that?" cried Tom.

Oliver stood silent cradling Tom. A mouse scurried by Oliver's feet, jumping up off the floor into one of many opened cupboards.

"You can get off of me now, Tom."

"I've had enough of this place. I'm off to reconnect with the cows."

They exited the kitchen and found what looked like the main bedroom. The quilt was cute, perhaps a little too flowery for their liking. There was something on one of the bedside tables.

"What is that?" asked Tom.

Oliver walked over towards the object and picked it up.

"It looks like a gas mask," remarked Oliver. Tom took the mask from Oliver and inspected it, adjusting the straps. He placed it over his head and breathed in and out, like a protagonist from a sci-fi movie.

"Take it off, mate. You look ridiculous."

Tom removed the mask from his head and threw it onto the bed. "Why would they need masks?"

Oliver thought for a moment. "You don't think it was because of NIFA do you?"

Tom scoffed, "Oh yeah, bloody NIFA. God, those masks were so bloody uncomfortable. My sunglasses used to fog up all the time."

Oliver sat on the bed and reminisced. "How many lock-downs did we have, you reckon?"

"A lot."

"People were going berserk."

"Yeah, every second night the news reported some dodgy idiot trying to break out of quarantine and across borders. It was mayhem."

"Thank goodness they were able to create a vaccine, hey?"

"Bloody hell, it took them a while though."

"The bugger kept mutating."

"I still can't understand why people were so anti-vax though?"

"Simple, because some thought that the government was forcing people to be vaccinated."

"Weren't they?"

"It was a medical mandate, not a forced vaccination. Big dif-ference. I remember my aunt spruiking that the government was taking her autonomy on what she could or couldn't do with her body. A few months later she was in a car accident."

"Oh, God! I'm sorry to hear, Ollie."

"It's ok. She survived, only just, but she killed a family of four on that fateful night."

"She killed them?"

"Yeah she was a drunk. She made a choice to down all those drinks of Tequila and get behind the wheel. She wanted her freedoms without the responsibility. She was only thinking about herself. She didn't care what happened to anyone else through her careless actions. It's the same thing as the vaccination argument."

"Fair enough, mate. Well, I got mine. I even got a lollipop," Tom grinned.

"It screwed the economy though. I reckon the virus set us back a good five or ten years. I mean, we're still using bloody Facebook. I would have thought we would be communicating via telepathy by now."

Tom chuckled.

"A lot of people died, hey?" said Oliver, massaging the back of his neck.

"Did you lose anyone, mate?"

Oliver stared at his reflection from the mirror. "Yeah, my sister."

"Ah, shit Ollie. I'm sorry to hear."

"It took everyone by surprise, didn't it?" said Oliver, his bottom lip quivering. "Anyway, life goes on as they say." Oliver wiped a single tear from his cheek and looked around the room. He noticed a dust-covered photograph on the floor.

"What's this?" asked Oliver, picking up the old photograph.

Tom came around the bed and looked at the photo. "They look happy."

It was a photo of a family of four; a mother, father, and two boys.

Tom snatched the photo from Oliver's hand. "Are they twins?" asked Tom, bringing the photo closer to his face.

"Yeah, looks like it."

Tom turned his attention towards the starred wallpapered wall behind the bed. "What on earth is that?" said Oliver. He stood and walked over to the wall and felt his hands down it. "It feels like a crack in the wall." Oliver grabbed one side of the bed. "Tom, grab the other side."

The iron-framed bed hardly moved.

"Far out this bed is heavy," exclaimed Tom.

"Are you doing anything, Tom?" grimaced Oliver.

"I was going to ask you the same thing, mate."

The bed slowly shifted away from the wall.

Tom held onto his knees and took deep breaths.

Meanwhile, Oliver inspected the hole and peered in.

"You see anything?" Tom asked, in between breaths.

"Nothing. It looks like a keyhole ."

"Where's the key?"

Both Tom and Oliver glanced around the room looking for signs of a key.

"There's got to be a key around here somewhere," said Oliver.

They opened the drawers of the bedside table and found nothing other than an aged Gideon bible. They looked under the bed. Nothing.

Tom opened the wardrobe.

"Anything there?" called Oliver.

Oliver held a lady's pink dress to his body. "You think pink's my colour?"

Oliver shook his head. He entered the en suite and opened the medicine cupboard. Inside there were two worn toothbrushes, a half-used tube of toothpaste, cotton buds, and several containers of prescription medicines. Oliver walked back into the main bedroom to find Tom trying on a woman's feathered hat. "Seriously, Tom. I wonder about you sometimes."

"What?"

"Come on, there's nothing here. Maybe it's just another wardrobe."

Tom threw the hat onto the bed and followed Oliver to the front veranda.

"We'll head back to the main road to try and find some help," said Oliver.

"Good idea. I'm bloody parched."

They walked off the veranda and onto the grassed field towards the road. They had only taken a few steps when Tom noticed something gleaming in the grass. He reached and picked up the shiny item.

"What the heck is this?" Tom asked.

Oliver inspected the item Tom had in his hand. "It looks like some sort of electronic card."

"Maybe it's an old part from a computer."

Oliver shook his head. "More like—"

"More like what?"

"Come on." Oliver ran back to the house.

"What now," said Tom, and ran after Oliver.

Oliver hurried into the main bedroom and stood at the wall.

Tom rushed in puffing. "All this exercise is seriously not good for my health."

"Where's that fob?" prompted Oliver.

"Fob? What the hell are you talking about?"

"The key, the key. Where's the key?"

"Isn't that what we're looking for?"

"Tom, the bloody shiny thing you have in your hand. Give it to me."

Tom handed Oliver the device and inserted it into the hole.

"Well, that was an anticlimax," announced Tom.

Oliver pushed and pulled the card into the hole several times. "What is wrong with this thing?"

"Maybe it isn't the key."

Almost ready to resign, part of the wall opened.

"Fuck me!" exclaimed Tom. "Where does it go?"

Oliver peered into the darkness. "I have no idea, let's find out, hey?"

Chapter 7

A few days later...

Aurora sat in her bedroom, brushing her hair. She was excited, but there was also trepidation. *What if I don't enjoy it?* Or worse, *how will mum react?*

There was a knock at the door. "Sweetie, can I come in?"

"Yeah."

Her mother entered the room. "Everything ok?"

"Yes."

Jasmine took the brush from Aurora and brushed long strokes of her daughter's hair. "I miss these quality times we have together, you know? It feels as though I hardly see you anymore."

"What do you mean? I'm either working into the night at the lab, or I'm at home." Aurora was irked by her mother's control. "I feel as though I know nothing about Cooinda, let alone any of my friends."

"That's not true. You see your friends almost every day."

"At work? You can't be serious?"

"What?"

"Why can't you let me enjoy my life?" replied Aurora, sullenly.

Jasmine stopped brushing and turned her daughter to face her. "Don't you enjoy your life?"

"I do. It just annoys me sometimes that I seem to be the only one, in my group of friends, without a social life."

"Sooner or later you'll realise that family is the most important thing in life, Aurora. Friends will come and go, but your family will be there through thick and thin."

Aurora turned to face the mirror. "Jake sort of asked me out tonight."

"Jake? From work?"

"Yes."

Jasmine pulled harder on Aurora's hair.

"You're hurting me!" exclaimed Aurora.

"Sorry," replied Jasmine. "So where are you two going?"

"Some festival."

"Festival? What sort of festival?"

"The Source Festival I think Jake called it. Why's that?"

"What about our girls' night in? I came to ask if you wanted to play virtual chess?" asked Jasmine, her smile brighter than usual.

"You're doing it again, mum."

"What?"

"Controlling me."

Jasmine sighed. "Ok, what about *Context?* You love playing that."

It was true, Aurora did enjoy playing Context. It was a video game that allowed her to interact with characters in various worlds. The best feature that she enjoyed was that the characters remembered what she had told them in the past. She often spoke to her virtual friends about her scientific drive but also her deep and often hidden emotions.

"Yeah, I do. But I want to actually meet real people, mum."

"And your father and I aren't real?"

Aurora sighed with frustration. "You don't understand. What did you do when you were my age?"

Jasmine pondered. "That was a long, long time ago, darling. Things were a lot different to what they are now."

"Really? I bet they aren't."

"Just promise me that we'll still have our girls' night now and then."

Aurora embraced her mother. "Of course. Right, so what should I wear?"

Jasmine put down the brush and placed it on the desk. She walked over to the wardrobe and scrolled through images of clothes displayed on the wardrobe doors. "Let's see. This one is nice," she said, pointing to a high neckline, grey suit."

Aurora sighed. "Why are all our clothes so bland?"

"Grey goes with so many things, though."

"Mum, can I ask you something?"

"Sure."

"Someone mentioned the other day at work that there's this conspiracy theory about some phantom element or something. Have you heard of this?"

"Phantom element?" said her mother, taking one of the many grey suits out of the wardrobe.

"Yeah, something about it causing disease and death," replied Aurora screwing up her face.

Her mother spun around. Her eyes narrowed and gave Aurora a piercing stare. "Who said this?" insisted Jasmine, her voice raised. "Was it Jake?"

"No, it wasn't Jake. Just some other guy." Aurora was caught by surprise by her mother's reaction. The look in her eyes was terrifying.

"See, this is exactly why I didn't want you to go out. There are too many crazies out there."

"Mum."

Jasmine's shoulders relaxed and gave a smile. "Sorry, your father hasn't been well lately and it's been playing on my mind. I shouldn't have snapped."

Aurora still felt scared. She had never seen her mother react as she did.

"So what did this person say?"

Aurora scratched her head. "Hayden's father had told him about this story that this phantom element was killing people and that we were moved to Cooinda to escape this thing."

"Hayden?"

"Yeah, just some guy from work. He's very immature."

"His father told him this story?"

"Yeah, so he says."

"Who's Hayden's father?"

"How on earth would I know? Why do you care anyway?"

Jasmine frowned. "I don't. It's just an odd story, that's all."

"Have you heard this story before?"

"Of course not," replied Jasmine, without hesitation.

"We would have remembered it though, wouldn't we? If it were true?"

"Yes, yes. That's right." Jasmine shook her head. "I think Hayden needs to stop telling these silly stories, to be honest."

Aurora looked at her ACCESS. "Jake will be here soon."

"Right, I had better get cooking." The door closed and Aurora laid back on her bed, reflecting on her bizarre experiences of late, starting with her odd dream, her invitation to the Source Festival, Hayden's odd conversation, and her mother's over-reaction. *Something isn't making sense,* she thought to herself.

About an hour later, there was a knock at the door.

Jasmine answered the door. "Hi, you must be Jake?" she smiled.

"Glad to meet you, Mrs Jemmerson," Jake replied.

"Come on in. Aurora! Jake is here."

Aurora walked downstairs and greeted Jake with a hint of a smile.

"Hi, Jake," she blushed. She could feel her device vibrate. She glanced at her wrist. Her heart was racing.

"You look great, Aurora. Is that outfit new?"

Aurora looked at her typical day-to-day attire. "Ah, no, I've had this for a while."

"Dinner will be ready in five minutes," called Jasmine as she proceeded into the kitchen.

"So, are you excited about the festival?" asked Jake.

"Ah, sure."

"Cool."

"Ok, guys, dinner is ready. Barry! We have a guest."

Everyone congregated in the dining room.

"You can sit here next to Aurora, Jake," prompted Jasmine.

The food was dished up with grilled salmon and home-grown potatoes on the menu.

"This looks fantastic, Mrs Jemmerson," said Jake, his eyes lighting up.

"You can call me Jasmine and it's my pleasure."

Barry interjected. "I watched a show about fish farms. It's the only reason we're not all vegans, you know?"

Jake nodded and took a bite of fish.

"Why do we rarely eat fish?" asked Aurora.

"Because we can obtain all our nutrients, vitamins, and

minerals from our fruit and vegetables," Jake replied.

"You seem to know your fair share about this, Jake?" said Jasmine.

"Yeah he's a crazy food scientist," laughed Aurora. She hadn't laughed for a very long time and she felt joy in being happy, even if for this moment.

"Are you?" said Jasmine, raising her eyebrow.

"Yeah, he's worked out how apples can make their own vitamins," said Aurora.

"Aurora, dear, let him answer," Jasmine interrupted. "Very interesting. So what are you working on at the moment, Jake?"

Jake swallowed his piece of fish. "I can't really say too much but this is very exciting," smiled Jake. "So we're combining physics, a little bit of chemistry, and molecular biology."

"Oh, sounds interesting," nodded Jasmine.

"Yeah, it is," said Jake, moving around in his seat. "So we have created these cells that can fuse oxygen and the elements get heavier until it reaches iron. These cells are then genetically modified into anything like lettuce, tomato, or even like this delicious looking potato."

"Right. Kind of like star—" Jasmine stopped short.

Everyone stared at Jasmine wondering what she was about to say.

"So tell me, Jake. What is Aurora like at work?" inquired Jasmine.

"She's fairly quiet actually. She's very focused on her work," responded Jake, piercing a carrot with his fork and taking a bite. "Oh, Mrs Jemmerson, this is delicious. Is that honey I can taste?"

"Thank you, Jake. Yes, it is. It's from SFC. I get a lot of products from them."

"What the heck does SFC stand for anyway?" said Barry, returning to the conversation. "Sounds like some sort of soccer club."

"Scientific Food Company, dear," replied Jasmine. "They make all sorts of genetically modified foods."

Barry grunted. "Could have added some of my home-grown Brussels sprouts though," added Barry. "I don't know about all this GMO garbage."

Jasmine smiled at Barry and then returned her attention to Jake. "Aurora tells me you're going to the Source Festival?"

Jake nodded. "Have you ever been to the Source Festival, Mr and Mrs Jemmerson?"

Barry and Jasmine exchanged looks. "Ah, I don't think so, have we, dear?" said Jasmine.

"Not that I can remember," replied Barry.

"It should be good. This year they have Groove Illusion playing," exclaimed Jake.

Jasmine rested her fork on her plate. "Aurora tells me that there's a story going around about some—, what did you say they called it, dear?" said Jasmine, looking at Aurora.

"Mum!"

"What? I'm just curious."

Jake took another bite of his salmon and watched Aurora.

"Well?" insisted Jasmine.

Aurora groaned. "Phantom element."

Jake stopped chewing. "Oh, that. Yeah, some story that Hayden believes." He shook his head and chuckled.

"See dear, it's just a story."

Aurora studied her mum's face and thought there was something her mother was keeping from her, before glancing at her wrist. "Oh, we had better get going. Doesn't the first act start soon?"

"Ah, yeah, we had better get going," said Jake as he completed his final bite of fish. "That was delicious, Mrs Jemmerson, ah, Jasmine. Thank you."

"Anytime, Jake."

Aurora stood and escorted Jake out of the house. Parked in the driveway was Jake's new ride. He opened the door by swiping his palm across the door sensor. "Not bad, huh?" said Jake proudly.

"Yeah. Nice car," replied Aurora.

"Hop in."

Jake raced around to the driver seat and announced, "Drive to Source Square." The navigation map drew the route and the car started and began its quiet journey to its destination.

"Wow. That's cool," said Aurora. "How does it know where to go?"

"The Source sends out low-frequency electromagnetic waves. There are heaps of repeaters around Cooinda."

"That's pretty neat."

"Yeah. Your parents seem nice," said Jake, admiring Aurora's profile.

"Yeah, they are," replied Aurora staring out the window and admiring the architecturally modern buildings. Now and then, the light emanating from the Source would fill the vehicle with its subtle blue hue.

"You mentioned once that you were home-schooled?" asked Jake.

"Yeah. My mum taught me everything there is to know."

"Cool. Yeah, I probably would have liked to have been home-schooled."

"Why's that?"

"I just think I would have been more focussed. Mind you, I made lots of friends at school and we went on some cool excursions."

"Where did you go?"

"One year we went to see what's underneath the Source. That was pretty interesting."

"Oh, yeah?"

"Yeah, it's incredible. It has huge containers of chemicals that produce oxygen. Heat generators from the fusion plant also supply light and energy for the city. All of this in one tower."

Aurora was impressed by how much pride Jake had for Cooinda and its technologies.

"This is good. I feel as though I haven't really gotten to know you properly," smiled Jake.

Aurora returned the smile.

"Does your mum and dad work?"

"Mum was a doctor and dad—. I'm not really sure what he did." Aurora was annoyed she didn't know as much about her father as she thought.

"Odd. How do you not know what your father did?"

"He's a complicated person," replied Aurora looking down at her feet.

"He's not the only one," mumbled Jake.

"What did you say?"

"I said you've got a great mum," replied Jake, his eyes darting between Aurora and the road.

"Hmm."

"Estimated time of arrival in two minutes," announced the car's navigation system.

"Enough about me. What's your family like?" asked Aurora.

"I have an older sister, Meg," replied Jake.

"What about your parents?"

"My mother lives about a block away from where I live."

"Your dad?"

Jake took his eyes off Aurora and looked out into the city. "He died just before I was born."

"Oh! I'm so sorry, Jake. How did he die?"

Jake hesitated. "I'm not sure."

"Anyway, let's not dwell on the past, we have a rocking festival to go to," replied Jake.

The vehicle slowed as it neared its destination. There were already thousands of people walking around. The thoroughfare led to a giant stage where the first act was finalising sound checks.

"How awesome is this?" shouted Jake, almost inaudible over the noise.

Aurora was taking it all in. An arm swung around Aurora's shoulder.

"Hey, guys!" It was Hayden and Crystal.

"Hi," replied Jake.

"Hi Aurora," said Hayden.

"Hi," she replied, moving away from Hayden.

"Are you going to introduce us to your friend?" asked Jake.

"Oh yeah, sorry. This is Crystal."

"Hi," smiled Crystal.

Aurora recognised Crystal in passing at work. They'd never properly met. Her first impression of her was that she wore too much makeup. It was the eyes that were the worst she thought. *Too much mascara.*

"So, ready for Groove Illusion? They're on in about two minutes," exclaimed Hayden.

The group walked closer towards the stage where people were chanting excerpts of Groove Illusion's songs.

The lights dimmed, except for the Source, which continued to flood the city with its light. Aurora felt exhilarated as well as nervousness having not experienced anything of this sort. All of her senses were heightened. There was chatter and laughter all around. She detected scents of different perfumes and colognes. She noticed Jake looking at her. He was visibly excited.

BOOM!

The crowd applauded in response to the sound of a bass drum.

"How are we doing tonight, Cooinda?" announced the lead singer.

The keyboardist started a motif, which the crowd instantly recognised and once again applauded. Three songs later, Aurora grew comfortable with her new surroundings. Her left foot occasionally stepped offbeat.

"Alright, Cooinda. One more song before we have a break. We hope you have enjoyed the concert so far. This song is special to me. It's about feeling lost. Feeling alone. Wanting to explore. But it's also about hope. Hope for a brighter future. This song's called Phantom Element."

Aurora's mouth fell open and the colour drained from her face. She felt dizzy and clammy.

"Hey guys, I might go and get some fresh air. I'll be right back," Aurora mumbled into Jake's ear.

Jake bobbed his head in time to the music.

Aurora stumbled her way through the sea of people hoping that there would be a break. If anything, the crowd thickened. Aurora spotted a gap and took a huge breath in.

"Ugh. Finally."

She headed towards the Source and sat down at its base. "What am I doing here?" she sobbed, placing her head between her legs. After a little while, she stopped sobbing and felt relief. There was a feeling of warmth and tranquillity, which she had not experienced before. Perhaps it was the heat produced by the nuclear fusion process that occurred within the bowels of the Source.

After a few minutes, she heard a humming sound behind her. It was the elevator that ascended the Source every ten minutes almost to the top, offering expanding views of the city. Aurora joined the queue to inspect for herself. Partly out of curiosity but also in delaying her return to the concert.

"Go on in," the robot instructed.

The line was surprisingly short. *Perhaps everyone else was enjoying the concert*, she thought.

Aurora stepped into the elevator, along with about twenty other people. The doors closed, and the carriage ascended at speed resulting in nervous laughter from the group. Aurora clenched her teeth in fear. It was only fifteen seconds until the elevator reached the top.

"Oh wow, what a view," some of them cried. Aurora was relieved to be out of the elevator and into the fresh air. She started her lap of the observation tower. Naturally, she looked in the direction of where she lived. She could just make out the Fairweather monorail station. She felt in awe of the many thousands of houses and streetlights that dotted the city. Turning farther clockwise she could see the business district, including the Trophtec laboratory, which camouflaged into the surrounding architecture. She inspected the digital plaque in front of her.

Welcome to Cooinda, home to twenty thousand inhabitants, all of whom were born here. Cooinda covers an area of approximately ten square kilometres. We, the people of Cooinda, thank William McPherson for his ingenuity and our beautiful city.

Aurora scratched her head. "How did they get here? And who gave birth to William?" she muttered.

Moving clockwise again she could make out the more affluent suburbs. Drenton and Castern. Aurora was fairly certain Jake resided in Castern. He had mentioned its specialty stores in previous conversations.

She saw children playing in one of the green spaces next to the McPherson building. She decided to take a closer look and eyed up to one of the permanent telescopes erected on the observation tower. The children looked so free-spirited. She could almost hear them laughing as they poked their heads from around the tree.

Aurora stepped back from the telescope and her forehead formed distinct creases. *Something is odd about that tree,* she thought, but she couldn't quite place where she had seen it before.

After almost an hour of taking in the sights of the city, Aurora could no longer hear sound from the concert and decided to ride the elevator back down. She doubted the rest of her group would have missed her. She decided to make her way towards Castern to better inspect the gardens.

Groove Illusion left the stage after their third encore. By all accounts, it was an epic act. Jake turned around to find Aurora to gauge her impressions of the show.

"Hey, guys! Where's Aurora?" said Jake with a degree of consternation.

The group looked around, obviously having not noticed her

absence either.

"I don't know," responded Hayden.

Jake led the conga line out of the crowd towards the Source.

"She can't have gotten too far," called Hayden.

The group looked everywhere within the festival's demarcation, including the Source observation tower. Nothing.

"I guess she thought you were a boring date and ditched you," said Hayden to Jake, laughing.

"Thanks," replied Jake.

"You're welcome," smiled Hayden. "Hey, I might go home too. See you around."

Hayden and Crystal walked off hand-in-hand, leaving Jake alone.

"I wonder where she went?" pouted Jake.

Chapter 8

Aurora rode the monorail towards Castern, eager to properly inspect the mysterious gardens. As she retreated from the city centre, a stranger sat beside her.

"Hello," said the stranger.

Aurora looked at the stranger and noticed it was a humanoid robot.

"Ah, hello," smiled Aurora.

"I sense that you are lost."

"Ah, no, I'm going to Castern."

"No, I mean, I sense that you're confused with who you are and where you are."

Aurora was perplexed. *How would a robot know this about me?* Her mother had told her how advanced robots were and that they could detect and emanate human emotion. "Do I know you?" she asked.

"No, I don't think so. I'm Roberto," said the robot, offering his hand.

Aurora shook the robot's hand. "Glad to meet you, Roberto. I'm Aurora. Do you travel on the monorails often?"

"No, I'm returning to my master's. I went to the festival. Did you go?"

Aurora glanced out the window, watching the city wiz by.

"Yes."

"Did you not like it?"

"I, I did. But I, I don't know, it was—"

"Too loud? Yes, I thought so too. My aural detection device was in overdrive," laughed the robot.

Aurora looked at the robot's face and smiled.

"Castern station," the voice-over announced.

"This is my stop." Aurora didn't want to leave. She felt an immediate connection with the robot but also wanted to inspect the gardens. "Thanks for your company."

"My pleasure."

Aurora disembarked from the monorail.

"Aurora, never stop searching," said the robot as the doors closed and the monorail continued.

Aurora exited the station and looked to her left towards McPherson Parade. She could make out the gardens from where she was standing. She walked towards the garden, passing several people on the way. Aurora picked up on the way they spoke. It was more eloquent.

"Oh, you don't say," said one.

"Indeed," was the response.

Aurora didn't recall hearing Jake speak in this manner.

She crossed McPherson Parade into McPherson Gardens. Situated out front was a large hologram of William McPherson. "Everyone seems to love this guy," she muttered.

On the other side of McPherson Parade was the garden. The children by this stage had long gone. There was little activity other than a loved-up couple sitting on a park bench, arms intertwined like a saprophyte strangling its host. Her presence had been sensed, and the couple walked away, intermittently looking back at Aurora.

"Well, this is tranquil," she said to herself. She walked to the lone tree in the corner. It was humongous.

"Oh wow!" Aurora exclaimed, bringing herself to a stop at the base of the tree. She touched the red cinnamon coloured bark. It felt scaly. There was an almost familiar smell that permeated the air. She noticed some fallen branches on the ground and picked them up and held them up to her nose. "Wow, it smells so, so fresh." She inspected the branch and noticed a small blue coloured flower. *This looks like—*

"Aurora!" came a call.

Aurora was taken by surprise.

"Aurora!" This time, with vibrato. "What are you doing here?"

"How did you know I would be here?" Aurora was suspicious. "Are you stalking me?"

"Stalking you?" laughed Jake. "No, I live just around the corner. I walk past these gardens every day to and from work. I drove home and needed some fresh air. Anyway, what are you doing here? And why did you leave the festival? Didn't you like it?"

Aurora felt silly in feeling paranoid. "I'm so sorry, Jake. I did. I just needed some alone time."

Jake didn't look convinced but didn't pursue it.

"Ok, why don't you come back to my house and we can get to know each other a little better, seeing that we didn't really have a chance at the festival?" said Jake.

"No, thanks. I'd rather just be alone if that's ok?" Aurora replied.

"What's going on, Aurora?"

Aurora looked up at the giant tree canopy. "I don't know." Her ACCESS vibrated. *You are feeling confused.* "Stupid thing."

"What's stupid?"

"Never mind. Hey, can I ask you something?"

"Yeah, sure anything."

"When did you first hear about that story?"

"What story?"

"The story that Hayden told."

"Oh, not that again. Why are you so hung up about that story?"

Aurora's attention shifted to Jake. "I don't know. There's something weird about it?" she replied, clutching her necklace.

They heard a knock. It sounded distant, but it increased in intensity.

"What the?" cried Aurora attempting to discern its location.

Jake's eyes widened and he scanned the perimeter. "It sounds as though it's coming from over there," pointing towards the giant tree.

Aurora checked whether anyone else had heard the knocking. There was no one else around. It was late at night.

Jake grabbed hold of Aurora's arm. "Stay close to me," he ordered.

Aurora hadn't realised Jake's touch. Her attention was instead focused on the knocking.

And then the sound stopped.

"Perhaps it's kids playing?" said Jake. "Hello! Is anyone there?" called Jake.

Aurora looked at Jake, thinking how absurd it is that Jake was calling out to an inanimate object. "At this time of night?"

They looked the tree over. There was nothing out of the ordinary. Aurora estimated the base at least three metres in diameter. She tilted her head back to inspect its foliage. In doing so, she almost lost her balance. The canopy spread from one side of the park to almost the other, obscuring much of the light from the Source.

"It's so beautiful, don't you think?" asked Aurora, her eyes drawn to the magnificent blue flowers.

"I guess," Jake replied.

"It's just like the one that's in my necklace," smiled Aurora. "And just like the tree that I saw in my dream—" Aurora's expression changed from admiration to fear.

"It's getting late. You sure you don't want to come home with me?"

"Huh? Ah no, I think I might go home now."

"Ah yeah, sure, ok. I'll walk you to the monorail." Jake gave a salute to the hologram of McPherson before leaving the garden.

"Why is it that we never see the guy?"

"Who?"

"The guy you saluted."

"McPherson?"

"Yeah."

"What do you mean, he appears regularly."

"You mean him as a hologram and his voice booming over the city?"

"Yeah, exactly."

"Have you ever seen him in person?"

Jake stroked his chin. "No, but he's probably a busy guy."

"You don't think it's odd that we've neither of us has ever seen him?"

Jake shrugged. "Not really."

Walking down McPherson Parade, they passed a queue of people almost two hundred metres long.

"What's going on here?" Aurora asked.

"I'm not really sure," replied Jake.

They followed the line that wrapped around the corner onto Banks Drive. Banks Drive led to the back entrance to Cooinda's museum.

Constructed nearly ten years ago when Cooinda was founded, it was a piece of architectural ingenuity. Inside, the design was configured as a circle with a conveyor belt carrying patrons around, starting and finishing at the same place. What was most intriguing about the design, was its ability to morph into various themes. The press of a button on a computerised screen altered the layout. The only static display was the McPherson display, in honour of the Cooinda's founder.

Finding the start of the line, Jake asked one of the eager line participants. "What is going on here?"

The young girl was completely oblivious, too preoccupied with taking photos of the museum using only her gloved hands. Capture was the latest craze of Cooinda. The kit came with wireless gloves that connected to the user's ACCESS. The user held up their hands to frame the desired subject and called, 'Take photo.' A photo was generated and stored on the user's wrist device.

Jake asked again, "Excuse me, what is going on here?"

This time the young girl heard Jake. "Oh, it's a special opening of a new display at the museum."

Jake looked towards Aurora and asked, "Do you maybe want to check it out?"

Aurora looked at her wrist device. It was almost midnight and she had ten missed calls from her mother.

"Nah, I'll head home, I think. You can go if you like, though."

Jake lowered his head.

"Oh look, why not," said Aurora. She felt guilty that she had skipped out of the concert earlier.

Jake's face immediately lit up and he raced back around the corner to the end of the line, with Aurora in tow.

After fifteen minutes of continual shuffling, Jake and Aurora neared the entrance to the museum.

"Hi, welcome to the Freedom display," said the robot concierge.

"The Freedom display?" said Aurora, to Jake.

Jake shrugged.

Passing through the doors, a spectrum of lights washed over them in a fan. They could feel the low bass and cacophony of high-pitched brass sound resonating off their bodies. Aurora looked at Jake, who was beaming with delight. She couldn't comprehend why but the mix of the light and sound made her feel at ease. They stepped onto the conveyor belt taking them to the first display. The sign outside the display read, 'The Simple Pleasures.'

Jake took Aurora's hand and led them off the conveyor belt into the display.

"Wow! This is incredible," exclaimed Jake.

Videos played of the people of Cooinda walking around the gardens enjoying themselves. They were laughing and playing games. She felt a sense of joy in seeing their freedoms.

The next display was interactive. Guests played with various inventions of Cooinda, including a prototype of the next model of ACCESS. They watched a video on upcoming Artificial Intelligence programs.

Aurora stood mesmerised. "Incredible. These machines can screen thousands of chemicals, found in our plants, to find suitable active ingredients for drugs to treat everything from cancer to autoimmune disease, " she whispered to Jake.

"Yeah, amazing isn't it?"

"You don't think that it's going a little too far, though?"

"What's the worst that could happen?"

"Ah, they could take over our life."

"Don't be ridiculous, we're in control of our own lives."

"Thanks to William McPherson, every citizen can enjoy life's luxuries without the exchange of currency or barter," announced a voice-over, synchronised with a montage of people enjoying a meal around a table. "You decide how much you want to work. In return, you receive time credits to ask the Divine your questions," continued the voice.

"That reminds me, my Divine day is tomorrow," said Aurora to Jake.

The conveyor belt moved to the next display, which was titled 'Creating a Better Future'. The screens flashed videos of William McPherson talking with people in the streets of Cooinda.

"He seems nice don't you think?" asked Jake.

"I guess," replied Aurora, inspecting designs of his, displayed on an electronic screen.

"He was so ahead of his time," said Jake with a grin.

"What's this?" Aurora inspected a glass cabinet containing various items that belonged to McPherson.

"Looks like some spectacles, a really old computer, and some sort of weird-looking thing that looks like it would go over your face. Looks pretty uncomfortable."

The room fell into complete darkness and along with it, all video and sound ceased, apart from the chatter of confused people around them.

"What is happening? I can't see anything." Aurora for once

reached to find Jake's hand.

"I'm not sure, hopefully, it'll come back on soon," replied Jake.

"Attention! There has been a malfunction. Emergency egress lights will soon illuminate. Please follow these lights towards the exit in an orderly fashion," boomed a monotone voice from above.

The emergency lights illuminated and people moved towards the exit.

Aurora was petrified. She hated the dark, as well as not feeling in control. "Jake, get me out of here."

"Calm down. We'll be out of here shortly. I've got you, ok?"

They snaked around passageways and touched their way through darkened rooms before they found the exit where Aurora took a deep breath and exhaled.

"That was scary!"

"It's alright. I wasn't going to let you go."

Aurora smiled but was still shaking from the experience. "I think I better get home. I've had enough adventure tonight to last a lifetime, I think."

Jake let go of Aurora's hand. "I'll see you tomorrow?"

"Yes, but I'll be a little late as I have my Divine day."

"Ok. I'll walk you to the monorail station if you like?"

"I'd like that."

Jake walked Aurora to the monorail station and waved her goodbye as soon as the monorail arrived.

Chapter 9

Tom peered down the abyss and shouted, "Hello!"

The hole responded with a diminishing echo, "Hello….ello….llo….lo,"

"What on earth is it?" asked Oliver.

"I have no idea," replied Tom.

"I think we should find out where it leads to."

"Good idea," said Tom. "You go first, I'll be right behind you."

Oliver wasn't convinced of Tom's commitment. "Fine."

Oliver took his phone from his pocket and attempted to illuminate the darkened passageway. "There are stairs," he called.

Oliver made his way down the stairs.

"Good work, Ollie. You're going well there, mate." Tom said encouragingly.

"Are you coming?"

"Ah yeah, mate. I'm right behind you." Tom apprehensively clambered down the stairs. "Man, it's dark," he cried. "How far down does this thing go?"

"We've only just started."

The stairwell was eerily quiet apart from Tom's heavy breathing.

"Maybe we should call for help," said Tom.

"It'll be fine mate, I'm sure it's just an old basement storing machinery and possibly food for your beloved cows."

"Yeah, yeah, you're probably right," replied Tom looking for any positive explanation.

THUMP!

"What is that?" gasped Tom.

"It's a wall," replied Oliver.

Oliver placed his hands on the wall and felt around. The wall was cool to touch but rough like the bark of a tree. "Odd. Why would they have a secret passageway that leads to a wall?"

"No idea, mate." And with that, Tom started his way back.

"Where you going?" cried Oliver.

"What do you mean? We're done. We discovered the hole and found a wall. Mystery solved."

"What is wrong with you?"

"Nothing, just that we're done looking around here."

Oliver knocked on the wall.

KNOCK! KNOCK! KNOCK!

"You hear that?" cried Oliver.

Tom was by this stage halfway back up the stairs.

"It sounds hollow."

KNOCK! KNOCK! KNOCK! KNOCK!

"Tom! I think it's a door!" Tom was by now back in the safety of the room. "Tom!"

Oliver felt around the wall again, looking for any signs of a door. He shone his phone onto the wall, sweeping from top to bottom, left to right. Unable to see anything, he made his way back up the stairs towards the room, finding Tom perusing through the bedside drawers. He closed shut the doorway, which gave a loud *thud*.

"Right, I think I've seen enough. Might try to pick up a ride and get some help with our 4WD," announced Tom, throwing a dog-eared newspaper dated 11th January 2030 onto the bed.

Oliver picked up the newspaper. "Where did you find this?"

"Over there," replied Tom, pointing to a corner of the room.

"January 2030. That's like ten years ago," pondered Oliver. He read the front-page headline, *NIFA: THOUGHT TO HAVE BEEN RELEASED BY A PHARMACEUTICAL COMPANY.* "Journalistic sensationalism at its best," he muttered, throwing the newspaper onto the bed.

"Is this true?"

Oliver shrugged. "I don't know, I find it hard to believe. I mean, why would anyone want to deliberately harm people for their own gain?"

"Yeah, you're probably right. Anyway, I'm off to chat to Betsy."

"Betsy?"

"The cow, of course."

Time had passed and the sun began to set over the sun-kissed land. Tom and Oliver walked out of the house and onto the veranda.

"Wow, check out those hues," called Tom, pointing towards the west.

"You surprise me at times, Tom," laughed Oliver.

"What?"

Oliver stroked his chin, thinking of what their next plan would be. He inspected the service bars on his phone. Still nothing. "I think I need to find a better provider. Let's go back down towards the road and wait for someone to pass by."

"Yeah, good idea, Ollie."

The two walked back towards the road, this time down the hill, which was a good thing as they were exhausted and hungry.

The cows had retreated to a shed estimated to be about four hundred metres to the west of the house.

They had only waited five minutes by the side of the road before headlights popped up over the horizon from the north.

"I think it's a car!" exclaimed Tom.

The lights got brighter.

"That's not a car! That's a road train!" exclaimed Oliver.

The truck engine roared as it approached.

Tom raced onto the road yelling and shouting, "STOP! HERE! STOP! HELP!"

"Get off the bloody road, Tom! It'll run you over like a pancake."

Tom ignored his friend's heed. "STOP! HELP! STOP!"

The engine changed notes, only lower. The truck was fast approaching.

Oliver leapt onto Tom, tackling him off the road and onto the curb. The truck rumbled past.

"Dammit, Ollie!" Tom yelled, reaching for his Akubra hat that had come loose.

"Oh, right! I just bloody saved your life and the best compliment you can give me is, 'Dammit, Ollie'," sighed Oliver, getting to his feet and dusting off his pants.

The rear lights of the truck disappeared over the horizon, along with the noise from the engine.

"Well, that's it then. We're done for," cried Tom, as though he had just experienced twenty days on an island on a reality TV show.

Just as Tom was devising a plan of cannibalism, the familiar sound of the truck engine could be heard in the distance. And then the blinding headlights reappeared.

Tom got to his feet, this time, however, remaining on the side of the road. The long, cattle truck slowed and stopped short of Tom and Oliver. They looked up towards the passenger door, which opened.

Tom looked towards Oliver. "Should we get in?"

"Would you rather stay here?"

"Good point."

They approached the truck and peered around the opened door. Inside was a very butch-looking woman, wearing a tight blue singlet.

"Hi there," greeted Oliver.

"G'day love! What are you two doing out here with nowhere to go?" replied the driver.

"Ah, well, see our ride broke down and we walked to find help," replied Tom.

"Well, you found it. What say you two get in and I'll take you into town?" responded the driver, displaying a grin with a few missing teeth.

They hesitantly climbed into the truck and closed the door, uncertain if this was their last ride.

The engine revved and completed a U-turn towards Quilpie.

"So I'm Dialla, you can call me Di."

"Hi Di, I'm Tom, and this is Ollie. You can call me Tom, and him Ollie."

Di laughed. "I'm beginning to like you already, Tom."

Tom shuffled towards Ollie, almost sitting on top of him.

"So, what brings you out this neck of the woods anyway?" asked Di.

Ollie proceeded to respond, but Tom interjected, "He's an archaeologist," pointing to Oliver.

"Oh? Like Indiana Jones?" exclaimed Di.

"Who?" Tom said with a perplexed look upon his face.

"Never mind."

"Yeah, ok— anyway, we're looking for fossils," added Tom.

"Yeah, well, there are plenty of those out here. Reptile as well as human," Di laughed again. Every time she did so, she would end with a snort.

"You got anywhere to stay the night?" asked Di, momentarily taking her eyes off the road and winking at Tom.

"Ah yeah, pretty sure we have friends in Quilpie, don't we, Ollie?"

Oliver, for the first time, entered the conversation, "Ah yeah, we're alright, thanks."

"So, you see anything interesting in that house?" asked Di, this time not taking her attention off the road in front of her.

"The house?" fumbled Tom. "What house?"

"The house you were outside of when I picked you up?"

"Oh, that house. Yeah, we just went to see if there was anyone there, but it looked deserted."

"Hmm," responded Di.

Di switched on the truck's radio, turning the dial.

"Say, do you like country music?"

Both Tom and Oliver watched Di fiddle with the radio before stopping upon hearing a country song.

"How old is that thing?" Tom asked.

Di laughed and snorted again, "Oh, this thing? Yeah, it is probably a bit of a fossil too, truth be known, but hey, it works."

The town lights could be seen up ahead. By this stage, the conversation had gone quiet, much to Tom's relief. The truck slowed as it approached Quilpie.

"So where should I drop you boys off?" asked Di.

Tom replied, "Here will do."

"You staying at the cemetery?" Di laughed.

Oliver looked out the window and could just make out a row of tombstones. "The nearest hotel will do, thanks Di."

Di just smiled. The truck pulled into the Quilpie Motor Inn, and the boys got out as expeditiously as they could.

"Thanks, Di!" Tom yelled, waving to Di as she exited the car park.

Oliver opened the front door of the motel and approached the front desk.

"How ya going?" inquired the receptionist of the hotel, who doubled as the chef judging by the flour-dusted apron she wore.

"Hi, we would like to stay for the night, if there are any rooms available?" asked Oliver.

"You're in luck, lads. We have just one more room left, and it has two beds. It's the ocean view suite."

"Ocean view!" exclaimed Tom.

Both the receptionist and Oliver laughed.

"You're travelling light too, I see?"

"Ah, yeah, It's a long story," replied Oliver.

"Righto guys, your room is down the corridor and the last room on the left. The kitchen is just about to open, so when you're ready, come on down and grab yourselves some tucker."

The receptionist handed the boys the key and readjusted her apron in anticipation of preparing a feast.

The boys found their room and simultaneously collapsed onto their beds.

"Not the most comfortable but at least we're out of that creepy house," groaned Tom.

Oliver didn't respond. He was already fast asleep.

"I guess we aren't eating tonight," remarked Tom, turning off the light.

Chapter 10

Instinctively, Aurora got to her feet as the monorail approached Fairweather. She exited the station and walked down Princeton Street. Approaching her house, she noticed the silhouette of a man peering into her lounge room window. She scurried behind a car that was parked opposite her house.

"Shit," she muttered. She looked at her ACCESS and typed the message *Mum there is someone outside our house. He's looking in thru the lounge window. Luv Aurora.*

Before she could press send, a man appeared by her side.

"Hello. Can I help you?" said the man.

Aurora's heart missed a beat. "Oh, far out. Where did you come from?" she said still crouching.

"Is everything alright, miss?" asked the man.

Aurora got to her feet. "Ah, yes thank you." She looked towards her house where the darkened figure was.

She attempted to discern the stranger's physical attributes, however, the dark concealed his face. She noticed that he was tall and wore a black cloak. It stood out, as no one in Cooinda wore black.

"I'm just checking on the area. There were reports of a disturbance around here," said the man while flashing an unrecognisable form of identification to Aurora.

"Oh, really? What sort of disturbance?" asked Aurora, attempting to get a closer look at the stranger.

"I'm afraid I can't divulge that information, miss." The man pointed to Aurora's house. "Do you live here?"

Aurora's eye's narrowed. "Ah, no, I live down the street. I tripped. Damn lighting around here is terrible."

The man grunted. "Indeed," he said, looking towards Aurora's house. "Anyway, everything seems to be in order now."

Aurora nodded.

The man opened his car door by pressing his hand against the sensor and started the ignition. The door closed.

"Where did you say you worked again?" Aurora asked, her voice muffled through the closed window.

"I didn't," he replied, before driving off.

Aurora stood in front of her house still unable to move. She could feel her heart pounding in her chest. She looked at her shaky hands. "This night just gets weirder and weirder," she said to herself.

Allowing her breathing to slow, she walked to her entrance and willed for the door to open. "Hello, Aurora," announced Nigel.

"Aurora, is that you?" called her mother.

"Ah, yes mum."

Jasmine welcomed Aurora in the lounge room.

Aurora was still shaking.

"Are you ok, dear?" asked Jasmine upon seeing Aurora's expression.

"I'm not sure," she replied.

Jasmine took Aurora's hand and sat her on the couch. "What's wrong? Was it Jake? I knew you shouldn't have gone out."

"Mum."

"It's too soon for you to be socialising."

"Mum."

"What?"

"It wasn't Jake."

"Was it the festival?" asked Jasmine inspecting her daughter's arms and checking her pupils.

"No! The festival was fine. Well, sort of." Aurora shook her head. "This night has been crazy and I don't even know where to begin."

Jasmine stood and hurried into the kitchen and fetched Aurora a glass of water.

"Here," said Jasmine handing Aurora the glass. "Start at the beginning."

Aurora finished the water in a single gulp. "I don't know how to explain it, mum."

"Explain what?"

Aurora handed her mother the empty glass. "I don't know what it is but I keep getting these weird premonitions and experiences lately."

Jasmine caressed her daughter's hands. "Maybe you're just under a lot of stress at the moment at work?"

Aurora shook her head. "No, it's more than that. It's like the universe is trying to tell me that there is more out there. I just can't work out what that is."

"I see," replied Jasmine.

"Aurora?" said Barry, rubbing his eyes. "What time is it?"

Jasmine let go of Aurora's hands and walked towards Barry who was halfway down the stairs. "Come on love. Time to get you to bed. In fact, I think it might be time for all of us to get some rest," she said looking at Aurora.

Aurora sighed. At the same time, she felt her ACCESS vibrate. *Message unsent.*

Aurora jolted upright. "Mum, was there a disturbance around here, earlier?"

"You go to bed dear, I'll be right there," said Jasmine to her husband. She walked back down the stairs towards Aurora. "What sort of disturbance?"

"I don't know. A man was looking through our lounge room window. He saw me and approached me. He said he was checking the area as there had been a disturbance reported."

Jasmine frowned and took a seat beside Aurora on the couch. "Wait, a man was looking through our window?"

"Yes."

"What did he look like? Did he say his name? Where he was from?"

"I don't know. Mum, you're scaring me, now."

Jasmine put her hand on Aurora's arm. "I'm sorry, dear. It's just very odd that someone would be looking through our window. Why wouldn't they introduce themselves to us and ask us directly?"

Aurora let her mother's words sink in. She felt fear and then annoyance in her carelessness. *Why hadn't she asked his name? Why hadn't she properly checked his identification?*

"I, I don't know, mum. One second he was peering through the window and the next he was beside me asking me questions."

"What sort of questions?"

Aurora's mind raced. "I, I can't really remember. Oh, he asked if I lived here?"

"What did you say?"

"Mum, I'm not that stupid. He flashed a badge but I didn't get his name. It was dark, mum. It was all very sudden."

Jasmine patted her daughter's arm. "It's ok. I might call the police tomorrow to find out. We'll talk more about this tomorrow, love. Come on, get some sleep," said Jasmine.

Aurora stood and walked upstairs to her bedroom and lay awake for some time before drifting off to sleep.

* * *

The next morning, Aurora awoke and got herself ready for work. She walked down the stairs and was greeted by her mother in the kitchen.

"Morning, dear."

"Morning," said Aurora.

"I've made fruit salad for you."

Aurora took the plate of fruit salad and gave it a sniff. "Smells good. Thanks, mum."

"What say we play a game of cards tonight when you get home from work? We'll have a family night."

Aurora bit into a strawberry. The juices dripped from her chin. "Sure," she replied.

There was a knock at the door.

Aurora walked to the door and opened it. "Hi, Jake. What are you doing here?"

"I was worried about you," replied Jake.

"Why would you be worried about me?"

"I don't know. It was just a really weird night last night. I wanted to make sure you were ok?"

Aurora blushed. "Oh, ok, sure." It was now Aurora feeling

the awkwardness of the conversation. "I'm ok. I don't mean to be rude but I'm kind of busy today."

"Oh, that's right. It's your Divine day, isn't it?."

"Yeah."

Jake grinned. "I can drive you to City Hall if you like?"

"Ah, ok, sure."

Aurora called out to her mother who was still in the kitchen. "Mum, Jake's taking me to the City Hall. We'll be back in a few hours."

Jasmine appeared at the door. "Hi, Jake."

"Oh, hello Mrs Jemmerson. Ah, sorry, Jasmine."

"Now I want you to keep an eye on her. Aurora's been under a lot of stress lately."

"Yes, of course, Mrs Jemmerson."

"Good." Jasmine gave her daughter a peck on the cheek. "See you soon."

Aurora closed the door behind and walked towards Jake's car.

They had only turned off Princeton Street before Jake spoke. "That was quite a night wasn't it?"

Aurora looked at Jake. "Yes, it sure was. It got even weirder too."

Jake took his eyes off the road momentarily. "Oh?"

"I got home and a strange man outside my house."

"A strange man?"

"Yeah, he said he was told to check on the area as there were reports of a disturbance."

"Odd."

"That's what I thought too."

"Did you tell your parents?"

"I told mum. She's going to call the police to check on it."

"Ok, good."

"I'm trying to make sense of everything that's been happening, but I can't."

"Well, a perfect opportunity for you today to find out."

"You have reached your destination," announced the car's navigation.

They stepped out of the car and admired the opulent-looking City Hall.

"It's been a while since I've been here," Jake remarked.

"Thanks for the lift, Jake. I'll be alright now."

Before Jake returned to his car, a chime was heard from above.

"Sounds like another death," said Jake. "I haven't heard the bleep to announce a birth for a few days, have you?"

Aurora shook her head.

A giant hologram of McPherson projected over the city. "Hello, Cooinda. I am sad to report that we have lost nearly twenty of our citizens to brain cancer in the last two weeks. We need further research to be done in this area. To this end, we, the Cooinda government, will be offering substantial rewards for those of you that can find a cure for this terrible, debilitating disease. As usual, your time working will be tracked. We will announce the fortunate citizen in a month. Thank you."

The hologram dissipated.

"There you go, Aurora. Haven't you already started working on glioblastoma?"

"Yes, but I want to finish the work on Granulomatosis first."

"I better get going. I'll see you later. Good luck with the Divine."

"Thanks."

"I think we should maybe catch up for dinner to talk things through."

"Maybe. I'll see you at the lab later today."

Chapter 11

Aurora walked into the grand entrance of City Hall and approached the giant touch screen. She was presented with various options including a *'City Hall Tour'*, *'Office Locations'*, and *'Ask the Divine'*. She selected the last option and a ticket with the letters A S was produced from the ticket dispenser. She removed the ticket and sat on the vacant couch and waited for her ticket to be called.

While she waited, she examined the hall's interior. She estimated the ceilings to be at least three stories high. There was no colour. The blackened walls absorbed any wavelength of light. Other than the touch screen, and the lone couch, there was no other furniture. *Where is everyone?* She had only been to this venue a handful of times, but every time she had, she felt uneasy. She could sense that her every move was being monitored. She counted at least twenty cameras sprawled around the building.

"A S, you may now proceed to the Divine Room," said a voice from above.

A row of green lights illuminated from the ground, paving the route to the Divine Room. Aurora stood and followed the path into an open-door room. Inside the room was a computer screen and a keyboard, similar to the one she had seen at the museum last night. She sat at the computer and read the instructions. It read, *Please scan your ACCESS.* Aurora did as instructed. The screen displayed her name and the amount of time she had in asking questions. *You have twenty-two minutes. The timer has started.*

The counter started counting down and Aurora started with her first question. *Where was William McPherson born?* she typed. The computer sat idle for a brief period before it displayed a response. *William McPherson was born in Cooinda.* She typed her next question, *Is William McPherson still alive? Yes,* came the response. "Succinct," she muttered. She typed in her next question. *What is reality?* Aurora tapped her fingers on the table waiting for the response. *Reality is simply a perception from the observer's point of view. None of what you see is real. The images you see with your eyes are nothing more than electromagnetic waves, arranged in your conscious mind, in such a way that it makes sense to the observer. The scents you smell are merely chemical reactions taking place in cells of your body and interpreted as defined smells. As such, the outcome of your reality is a result of any number of probable perceptions This means that your life's journey may take any number of paths, defined by your unconscious.* 'Wow. I'm not sure I completely understand what it means, but interesting," grinned Aurora.

Aurora checked the timer. "What? Two minutes remaining. Where did that time go?" She quickly pondered what her final question might be, before quickly typing her query. *Is there life outside of Cooinda?* The computer screen flickered. "What's going on?" she said to herself. The screen went blank. She could see a reflection of a figure on the blank screen. She swivelled her chair around and was faced with the man she had seen outside her home last night. "What, what are you doing here?"

"I see you're having issues with the Divine," said the man.

Aurora's throat was dry and her feelings of anxiousness returned. "Who are you?"

"My name is Arnold," replied the man.

"Why are you stalking me?"

Arnold chucked. "Stalking you? Don't be ridiculous. It's pure coincidence that I have come across you again."

No longer under the guise of the dark, Aurora could better discern the stranger's appearance. He was tall, with blonde hair. His eyes were hazel in colour, but evil-looking. She felt uncomfortable being in his presence. "What are you doing here?" she insisted.

"I'm here to fix the computer."

"How did you know it was broken?" replied Aurora, frowning.

"I monitor the system. It logged an operating system error and I came down straight away."

Aurora was suspicious. "Can you see the questions I ask?"

"Of course not. The system is incredibly secure. There are layers of firewalls."

"What exactly is your job?"

"I'm the principal security officer of Cooinda. My job is to ensure the safety and integrity of Cooinda and its citizens." His ACCESS vibrated. "Damn, I have to go. I'll fix the Divine later today."

"But I still I had two minutes remaining. I didn't receive my answer," Aurora galled.

"We will just credit that time over to your next day," replied Arnold, exiting the room.

Aurora stood up from the computer and left the City

Hall frustrated that her most poignant question hadn't been answered. She made her way, by foot, to the laboratory, which was a short walk away.

93

Chapter 12

Meanwhile, in Quilpie, the boys enjoyed a hearty breakfast of bacon, eggs, tomato, and some homemade hash browns. The receptionist, this morning the cook, stood at their table. "Morning fellas. How was your sleep?"

Tom, with a half-filled mouth of food, replied, "Yeah good thanks. Slept like a baby."

"So, where are you two off to today? Opal fossicking, or maybe you could head up to Baldy Top Lookout?"

"Baldy Top Lookout?" replied Oliver. "What sort of name is that?"

"Cheryl!" came a call from the kitchen. "We need more pancakes."

"I better get back to work. Have a fun day."

"Thanks. Oh, is there anyone that can maybe give us a lift back to our 4WD? It's just out of town. I think we might need a mechanic, though," asked Oliver.

Cheryl adjusted her stance and pondered. "Oh yeah, Mick is a mechanic. He should be able to help you guys out. He's our gardener too. I'll go find him."

As Cheryl walked away, Tom said to Oliver, "What is it with these people? They all work like two or three jobs."

Oliver shrugged as he took a bite of his crispy bacon. "Damn, this is good. I will never be a vegetarian."

The boys finished up their breakfast when Mike walked into the restaurant and approached their table. "G'day, boys! Mike's me name," he said, offering his hand.

"Glad to meet you, Mike," said Oliver, shaking his hand.

"Hi," added Tom, massaging his palm after shaking Mike's hand.

"Cheryl tells me that you've broken down?"

"Yeah, just out of town," replied Oliver.

"I'm surprised we made it this far," added Tom.

Oliver glanced at Tom disapprovingly.

"Righto. Well, you boys tidy up, and we'll head on out, hey?"

The boys checked out of their room and found Mike waiting beside his ute.

"Righto, hop on in," instructed Mike.

Mike Hislop was a big lad. Over six feet tall, broad shoulders, sun-bleached hair, and a chiseled face, which showed significant signs of sun damage.

The engine of Mike's ute turned over, and they made their way towards the abandoned 4WD.

"So what brings you two out here, anyway?"

Oliver looked at Tom, who was fixated on his surroundings.

"I'm into fossils and rocks," replied Oliver.

"Rocks, hey? Yeah, right, well you've come to the right place for that."

The sun rose quickly. Already the air was heating up. The abandoned house could be seen up ahead.

"Oh God," announced Tom.

"What's up mate?" asked Mike.

"That creepy house. There it is again," replied Tom.

Mike laughed. "Creepy house hey? I'm glad I'm not the only

one that thinks so."

They drove past the house and continued along the bitumen road that created a shimmering effect. The ute slowed to a stop as it approached the abandoned LandCruiser.

"Righto, pop the bonnet for me," requested Mike who got out of the car and walked to the front of the 4WD.

Oliver opened the bonnet. "What do you think the problem is?"

Mike pulled on tubing and leads. "Fan belt I'd say."

"You got a spare one?" asked Oliver.

"I do, but it's back in town," replied Mike, wiping his greased hands on his denim jeans.

"Great, first it was the radiator and now it's the fan belt," cursed Tom.

Mike looked at his watch. "Shit."

"What?" said Tom.

"Ah, nothing. I've got a few jobs I need to do for Cheryl. What say I leave you guys here with the car and I'll race back into town and grab that fan belt and you'll be on your way."

"We can't come back into town with you?" asked Oliver.

Mike shook his head. "I won't be long, lads. An hour at most." Mike handed two bottles of water to Tom and Oliver. "Here. You don't want to be stuck out here without any water."

Tom looked at Oliver. "No, you do not," he muttered.

"Hey, it wasn't my fault that the Beast was thirsty!" Oliver exclaimed.

Mike hurried to his vehicle and drove towards Quilpie at speed.

"There are some strange people around here," said Tom.

"Yeah, what could be so urgent?" asked Oliver.

"Maybe he forgot to water his roses?"

Oliver wasn't amused. "Let's get out of this sun. We'll head back to that house we went to yesterday."

"Oh no, not that creepy house, Ollie."

"It's fine. It's just old."

Tom moaned.

The sun was already past the midpoint in the sky when the boys walked up the familiar incline towards the house. This time though, there were no cows to be seen.

"I wonder where Betsy is?" asked Tom.

"You and your damn cows, Tom."

They stumbled onto the veranda. Both boys were heaving.

"That hill is like bloody Mt Kosciusko!" cried Tom in between deep breaths.

After both their heart rates had returned to normal, they walked into the house.

"This place really spooks me out, Ollie."

"It's fine. We will just sit here and wait for Mick to arrive. We should be able to hear it from here."

Oliver slumped into the sofa, giving rise to a cloud of dust. "Well, this isn't ideal."

"What isn't, mate?" said Tom.

"Well, we're supposed to be looking at fossils and rocks, not sitting in a run-down house."

"Correction. You're looking for fossils and rocks; I'm looking for chicks."

Oliver moaned. "You reckon it's a bit weird that both Mike and the woman that picked us up last night were acting strange about this place?"

"Ah, yeah, I guess. I don't know. I hadn't really thought much about it, to be honest." Tom poked his head outside the front door intermittently to locate the cows.

The day raced away and before they knew it, the sun was setting "This is flipping ridiculous! I don't think Mike is coming back," exclaimed Tom."

Tom had given up locating Betsy and joined Oliver on the sofa.

"Yeah, I think you're right. What are we going to do?" asked Oliver.

Oliver's train of thought was disrupted by a shallow-sounding thump. "What was that?" Oliver turned around in his seat, attempting to locate the source.

"I don't know, maybe it's the taps again," replied Tom.

THUMP! THUMP!

"There it is again," called Oliver. "It's coming from the bedroom."

Oliver leapt to his feet and walked towards the bedroom.

THUMP! THUMP! THUMP!

"Over there," called Tom, pointing towards the secret door. "It's coming from that passageway."

"Yep, I think you're right," replied Oliver, removing the electronic key from his pocket.

"What the hell are you doing, Ollie?" cried Tom. "Don't think that I'm coming with you this time."

Oliver inserted the key into the hole in the wall, opening the door. "Fine, you wait here and wait for Mick. I'm going to find out what this is."

Tom let out a sigh, "Fine, I'll come but if anything happens, I'm outta here."

Oliver illuminated the passageway with his phone and they made their way down the stairway holding onto the walls to steady themselves.

THUMP! THUMP! THUMP!

Tom could feel his heart beating hard in his chest and was almost piggybacking Oliver.

"Can you get off of me, Tom? I can feel you breathing down my neck."

"Sorry Ollie, I'm just not sure about this, hey?"

"It'll be fine. I'm sure there's a logical explanation for this. It's probably some piping that has come loose."

Their descent ended when they found themselves at the dead end.

THUMP! THUMP! THUMP!

Oliver pressed his ear onto the wall. "It's coming from this wall!"

Tom's teeth could be heard chattering, and he was now holding onto Oliver's waist. "I think we should go back up now, Ollie," whimpered Tom.

The entry door that they had just entered through closed shut.

"Shit! We're stuck in this hole," Oliver exclaimed. "Help! Help!"

"Would you get off of me!" yelled Oliver.

"Why did the door close?" screamed Tom.

"I don't know but you need to calm down."

Tom released his grip around Oliver, and outstretched his arms, and pressed them against the walls. As he did so, his hands gave way and the darkened passageway was alight.

Chapter 13

Aurora sat at her bench, at the lab, deep in thought. She hadn't heard Hayden enter.

"Hey, guys. Do you maybe want to go out tonight?" asked Hayden, picking up a pipette and playing with its plunger.

Jake glanced up from his bench, "Maybe?"

"Or you going to stand us up again, Aurora?"

"Hayden," piqued Jake.

"What? She did."

Aurora snatched the pipette from Hayden's hand. "You need to grow up."

"Someone's a bit sensitive today," Hayden mocked.

"Would you give it a rest, Hayden?" added Jake. "We can't."

Hayden shook his head. "We? Who's we?"

"Aurora and I just need to talk about some things."

"Fine, suit yourselves. I've got some important news to tell you all but I guess it'll have to wait."

"What sort of important news?" asked Jake.

Aurora rolled her eyes.

"Nah, You'll have to wait now," said Hayden, with a wink.

Jake looked at Aurora. "Maybe we should go."

"But what about us catching up?" said Aurora to Hayden.

"It can probably wait."

Hayden added, "I'm still here guys."

Aurora was agitated. "Fine. We'll go out and hear about your important news, but I need to be home early."

"Absolutely," replied Jake.

"Where we going anyway?" asked Jake.

"Illuminate," replied Hayden.

Jake loved Illuminate. It was his favourite restaurant. It was located across from Source Square. "Alright. See you at six."

Hayden left the lab and Aurora and Jake returned to their work.

"How was the Divine?" Jake asked Aurora.

Aurora's shoulders slumped. "Weird."

"Weird?"

"Yeah, I asked some questions and got odd responses, and when I asked the final question the computer died."

"What do you mean, died?"

"The screen went blank. It was like there was a power surge."

"Like last night?"

Aurora held onto Jake's words. "Exactly like that, come to think of it. It's like the universe doesn't want me to know the truth."

"That is weird."

"Want to know something even weirder?"

"What?"

"You know that man I was telling you about? Who was outside my house peering in?"

"Yeah?"

"He stood behind me."

"Where?"

"At the computer."

"Was he there the entire time?"

"No, no. Only when the computer went down. He said he was monitoring the system and was there to repair it."

"That is very weird. Is he stalking you or something?"

"That's what I said. He freaks me out. There's something odd about him."

"He's probably on something."

"Maybe."

"So do you want to talk about last night?"

Aurora turned her back to Jake and switched on the real-time PCR machine. "Not now. I have work to do."

"Fair enough."

* * *

A few hours later.

"We better get going. Hayden will be waiting for us," said Jake.

"Ok, I'm almost finished," replied Aurora. She placed flasks into the incubator and hung up her lab coat, before exiting the building along with Jake.

Outside, Hayden was waiting by the laboratory's front entrance.

"Right. Let's go," exclaimed Hayden.

Source Square was within walking distance of the lab. Hayden was visibly excited and was almost skipping his way towards the restaurant. The light from the Source was now a mauve-coloured luminescence, to match the time of the day.

Within ten minutes, the group arrived at the east entrance of the square. The stage from the festival was still being dismantled from last night.

"Hey, where did you go last night, Aurora? We were looking for you everywhere," Hayden quizzed.

Aurora hadn't a chance to respond before Crystal joined the group.

"You remember Crystal, don't you?"

Aurora sheepishly smiled and nodded. *Still too much mascara.*

The group walked to the western side of the Square, where there was a row of chic cafés and eateries. Illuminate was already popular with people mingling outside.

"Right. Here we are. I've made a booking for five, so we should be right to go right on in." called Hayden.

The front-of-house usher met them.

"Good evening, do you have a reservation?" asked the humanoid, not looking up from its screen.

"Yes, it should be under Hayden's Groovy Crew," replied Hayden.

Aurora bit her lip and shook her head.

The usher did not respond.

"Very well, follow me, please."

The group was escorted to their table. As soon as they were seated, a procession of staff arrived like a well-rehearsed scene from a theatrical play. Glasses were filled with water. Napkins were placed onto the guest's laps and menus were handed out.

Aurora scanned the menu. She had little appetite.

"What are you eating, Aurora?" asked Jake, leaning over her menu.

"I'm not sure. I'll probably just have the soup," responded Aurora.

"Everything alright?" asked Jake.

Aurora nodded. "Yes, everything is fine, just a little tired, that's all."

The waitress arrived at the table and started with Hayden, who was unsurprisingly famished, and ordered the largest item from the menu. The Extravaganza. It was a platter-sized plate of pasta and vegetables. It was an odd combination; however, it was considered the drawcard for Illuminate as very few people managed to finish the meal.

"I'll have the potato and leek soup," said Aurora when it came time for her order.

"I think I'll go the soup too please," said Jake.

"I'll have the potato gnocchi," grinned Crystal.

The waitress left with the orders.

"So how good was the festival last night?" Hayden said excitedly.

"Yeah, it's a shame you missed it, Aurora," said Crystal, while taking a sip of her water.

"Ah, yeah, sorry about that," Aurora replied.

"Where did you go, anyway?" asked Crystal.

"I just needed some space and found a park to sit in to relax."

"A park? Ok, cool Which park?" said Hayden.

"McPherson Gardens," Jake interjected.

"McPherson Gardens? What were you doing over there?" asked Crystal.

Aurora shrugged. She wasn't in the mood to make idle talk.

It wasn't long before the food arrived at the table and Aurora watched Hayden tuck his napkin into his shirt and picked up his knife and fork readying himself for his meal.

The plate of soup was placed in front of Aurora. She picked up her spoon and swirled her soup.

"You going to eat that, or are you just going to do a science trick?" Jake chuckled.

Aurora looked up at the rest of the group, all of whom were

occupied with their food.

"So what's your important news Hayden?" asked Jake pursing his lips to taste the hot soup.

Hayden had remnants of his food around his mouth. "Oh, yeah, that." He placed his fork and knife down on the table and licked his fingers. "So Crystal and I are engaged."

"Oh, congratulations," said Jake.

Aurora stopped playing with her soup and smiled. "Congratulations Hayden and Crystal." She then placed her napkin on the table and whispered into Jake's ear. "I have to go, I'm sorry."

"Oh, ah, you ok?" replied Jake.

"Yes, I just need to get home."

Aurora stood before saying, "I have to go. Congratulations again."

Aurora hastily walked towards the exit and stood outside the restaurant, bathed in the Source's light.

"Oh, for goodness sake. Not again," said Hayden, throwing his napkin onto the floor.

"Come on, Hayden, we had better go too," said Jake.

"Fine," said Hayden.

The group left the restaurant and found Aurora perched on a seat overlooking the Square.

"What's wrong, Aurora?" asked Crystal. "We're just concerned for you, that's all."

"Yeah, we are," replied Jake.

"Hey, nice necklace by the way," said Crystal.

Aurora looked down at her necklace and held it in her hands. "Thanks."

"What's inside?" asked Crystal.

Aurora unlatched the locket to reveal the flower.

"What is it?" asked Hayden.

"It's the Cooinda flower," replied Aurora. "The same flower I saw last night in the gardens."

"Yeah, from that tree that we heard noises from," exclaimed Jake.

"Huh?" replied Hayden. "You heard noises from a tree?"

Jake looked at Aurora, uncertain if he had said too much.

"Well, we should check this tree out then," replied Hayden. "The night is still young."

Aurora stood and frowned. "No, no, no. I need to get home." She looked at Jake and said, "I'll see you tomorrow at work."

"Aurora, wait," said Hayden, grabbing her by the arm. "Why don't we go to the garden? You said you feel relaxed there."

Aurora paused and reflected. "I do," she said clutching her necklace. "There's something about that place." She let go of her necklace. "But I need to get home."

"Come on, Aurora. Please?" begged Hayden.

Crystal gave Hayden a kick in the shin.

Aurora picked up her bag. "Fine. I'll show you this tree and then I'm out of there. No more excuses."

"Absolutely," replied Hayden.

They walked to the monorail station and waited for the monorail to arrive.

"So how long have you known Crystal?" asked Jake to Hayden.

Hayden studied Crystal and said, "I don't know actually. Maybe a month?"

Crystal nodded. "Yeah, I think so."

"Ah, ok. You don't waste any time do you?" said Jake.

The monorail arrived at the station and they made their way towards Castern. Arriving there, Jake led them towards

McPherson Gardens. Unlike the previous night, the place was deserted.

Aurora looked around until her gaze fixed on the large tree. She walked over to it and wrapped her arms around the broad trunk.

"What is she doing?" inquired Hayden.

"I'm not sure," replied Jake.

"This is the tree you heard noises coming from?" asked Hayden.

"Yeah. This is the one," replied Jake.

Aurora rubbed her hands over the bark and began tapping, lightly at first.

"You hear that?" cried Aurora.

"Hear what?" replied Jake.

Aurora began knocking again, this time harder.

THUMP! THUMP! THUMP!

"That. It sounds hollow," exclaimed Aurora.

The group made their way towards the tree.

THUMP! THUMP!

"See! It sounds hollow. I knew there was something odd about this tree," said Aurora.

Hayden was still not convinced and knocked on the tree.

THUMP! THUMP!

"Oh wow!" Hayden replied. "You're right! It does sound hollow."

Hayden pressed his ear against the trunk. As soon as he did, there was a loud creak, and the trunk revealed a doorway.

"What in Cooinda is that?" cried Jake.

Chapter 14

"Barry!'" called Jasmine. 'Barry, where are you?'

Jasmine looked for Barry all over the house. She found him attending to his garden, adjusting the trestle for his hydroponically grown beans.

"Ah, there you are," said Jasmine. I'm worried about Aurora."

Barry paused and looked up to his wife of thirty years. "Why?"

"She's been asking some curious questions. I think we need to tell her."

Barry picked off a leaf. "I think they might need more phosphorus. What sort of questions?"

"She said to me the other day that someone had told her a story about the phantom element."

"Phantom element?"

"Yes, that's what she called it."

"I have no idea what you're talking about, Jazz."

"I think that's a pseudonym for the virus."

Barry looked at Jasmine. "Virus? The one you told me about years ago?"

Jasmine played with her grey collar. "Yes, I think it might be the same one."

"What makes you think she knows about it though? You said

to me that you think only you know about the past?"

Jasmine nodded. "That's what concerns me. Someone from her work told her."

Barry shook his head. "You know kids, Jazz? Their minds are always running a mile an hour."

Jasmine looked towards the house to check if Aurora had returned from work. "I don't know, Barry. I've got a weird feeling about all of this. She said a strange man was looking through our window the other night, too."

"What strange man?"

"I don't know. She said he was responding to a disturbance."

"Probably me yelling at the soccer scores," huffed Barry.

"I hope it wasn't Arnold," said Jasmine. Her hands began to shake upon reflecting on her haunted past.

"Arnold? The same Arnold that tried to kill me?"

Jasmine nodded.

"The freak that was obsessed with you?"

"Yes, the same one, Barry," replied Jasmine, frustrated with her husband's inability to properly comprehend.

"But you took out a restraining order on him. He's not to be within a hundred metres of you?"

Jasmine looked at her hands. She felt faint. "Yes, I know. I wish he hadn't been selected to come here too."

"I don't understand. Why would he be looking for you after all these years?"

"I don't know." Jasmine shook her head in the hope that it would erase her memories of Arnold. "What are we going to say to Aurora?"

"Why don't you tell her about the outside world then?"

Jasmine shook her head. "I don't know. It's a big deal."

"I took it alright when you told me."

"Yes, but I think Aurora may not take it nearly as well."

Barry shrugged. "In some ways, I think that mutation you have is a curse. I'm glad I have no memory of the past by the way you described it. Sounds pretty bleak."

Jasmine's eyes began to well. "You have no idea," she said.

"That's true.

"It was probably a good thing that when we were injected with that drug most of us have absolutely no recollection of our past lives. For all we know they may still be suffering, or perhaps they're now all dead."

"How come I can remember how to write, read, speak and everything else?"

"I'm not sure. Perhaps the drug is specific for only memories of the past. I remember scientists working on a drug that erased memories of alcohol usage in alcoholics and nothing else. Maybe it's similar."

"At least I feel safer here for my health," smiled Barry.

"That's true, dear. We all just have to remember to take our daily pill."

"You mean *Synthacter*?"

"That's the one."

"Synthacter, cause your life matter," Barry sung. "It's a catchy little tune isn't it."

"Luckily I didn't marry you for your voice, dear," said Jasmine, hugging her husband.

"Terrible tasting vitamin," added Barry, pulling faces.

"Well, it's not actually a vitamin."

"It's not? But the ad on the television says it is."

"Call it misleading advertising."

"Well I'll be," replied Barry, expressing shock. "So if it's not a vitamin, what is it then?"

"It's synthetic bacteria."

"Synthetic bacteria? I thought you said Cooinda doesn't have any bacteria or viruses."

"It doesn't. Believe it or not, though, humans evolved with the need to survive with bacteria. Before we entered here, our guts contained billions, if not trillions of bacteria. They helped break down our food."

"What about now?"

"Well, Mr McPherson was adamant that he didn't want anything that could potentially harm us but we can't alter evolution overnight and so he gave us each an antibiotic each before we arrived and were told to take this drug daily. It's synthetic bacteria. They've taken the genes from bacteria and put them into nanoparticles. Pretty cool, huh?"

"Sounds like a science experiment gone wrong, if you ask me."

"Still, I'm glad we were fortunate enough to have been selected by McPherson's lotto."

Barry planted a bean sprout into the synthetic-soiled ground. "What was that lotto again?"

"I think that drug is still working, love," said Jasmine touching her husband's hand. "During the terrible pandemic, Mr McPherson advertised a lotto that Australians could enter. It was called the *'Once in a Lifetime Adventure'*."

Jasmine knelt on the ground, beside her husband. "I hated leaving my friends and family behind."

Barry gave Jasmine a pat on her shoulder. Jasmine hated the fact that Barry's affection was nothing like it was when she first met him. "I'm kind of glad I have no memory of them, to be honest."

Jasmine looked into the distance and reminisced on her past.

"Barry! Barry! We've been selected," yelled Jasmine, over the noise of the lawnmower.

"Selected for what?" replied Barry, shutting the engine off.

"To escape here and move to Cooinda."

"About bloody time. I'm not sure how much longer I could stand living like a hermit, in fear of catching this NIFA virus."

"Yes, I know. We just have to be tested and as long as we're negative and we have no other illnesses for fourteen days, we are good to go."

"How do we get there?"

"I'm not sure. The email just says that more information will be made available shortly. I'll go tell Aurora."

"Aurora, we're getting out of here."

"Where are we going?" Aurora replied, removing her hoverboard boots from her feet.

"To a better place. It's called Cooinda, which means Happy Place."

"Can Ellie come too?"

Jasmine stroked her daughter's cheek. "No, dear. She has to stay behind. Grandma and Granddad Stevens have to stay here too."

Aurora cried, "Why? I love them. I want them to come with us."

A tear fell down Jasmine's face. "I know, dear. I do too. We all do. But they can't."

"Will they die if they stay here?"

Jasmine tightly embraced her daughter. "I hope not. And hopefully, we will only stay there until it's clear for us to return."

"Do you promise?"

"I promise we'll see them again," smiled Jasmine.

Her mind raced forward a few weeks.

"Next," called a lady, standing at the front entrance of a colonial-style house.

A line of people snaked around a large paddock, in the dead of the night. The Jemmerson's approached the front entrance.

"Please show me your verification email," instructed the lady.

Jasmine showed the lady the email which confirmed their acceptance into Cooinda.

"Thank you," replied the lady, before presenting each of them with a wrist device. The lady then jabbed each of them with a needled syringe into their arms.

"What is that?" asked Jasmine.

"It's called Memezumab," replied the lady. "Not that'll mean much to you as none of you will remember any of this," she smiled. "Next!"

They shuffled through the door into their new world.

Jasmine returned to her current surroundings.

"I wonder what the authorities told them about our disappearance?"

"They told them that we had died from NIFA."

Barry looked at Jasmine and frowned. "So they don't know that we're still alive?"

Jasmine shook her head. "Of course not. Could you imagine if they told people that some of us have left to enter a new city free of all that shit? I think you're right, Barry. I think it's better we don't tell Aurora."

Chapter 15

"What the?" Aurora couldn't complete her sentence.

"I can't see!" cried Oliver.

"Who's there?" Jake called.

There was confusion all around as the two worlds united. Oliver took a step forward towards the light, his eyes slowly adjusting.

"Wait! Where are you going, Ollie?" called out Tom.

Oliver continued his awkward shuffle into the new world. Only a few steps were needed before he entered Cooinda, like a fetus exiting the birth canal, into its new environment.

The Cooinda group stepped back simultaneously as they watched Oliver slowly emerge from the doorway. Initially, there were no words spoken as each person attempted to comprehend what exactly was taking place. Oliver was the first to speak. "Where, where am I?" he asked as he scanned his new surroundings.

"Ollie. Wait for me," came the cry still within the tree.

The Cooinda group took another step back.

Tom hesitantly stumbled from the tree and joined Oliver. "What the hell is this place?" said Tom.

The doorway closed without a sound.

"I have no idea," said Oliver.

Jake managed a squawk, "Who are you guys?"

Everyone was silent for a bit before Oliver replied, "We're wondering the same thing."

Aurora ran to the tree and inspected the tree. "Where did you come from?" she said.

"Ah, from that tree," replied Oliver.

"Are there more of you?" insisted Aurora.

"Nope, just us two," said Tom.

Jake scratched his head. "Are you from another universe?"

Tom laughed. "I was going to ask you guys the same thing. I mean, look at this place. It looks like we've stepped forward in time."

Crystal went to reach forward to touch Tom's clothes before Hayden restrained her. "No don't touch them," she said. "We don't know anything about them."

Hayden kept Crystal close to her. "So maybe we should introduce ourselves. I'm Hayden. This is my fiancée Crystal."

"And I'm Jake."

"Glad to meet you all. Oh, I missed your name," said Oliver, looking to Aurora.

Aurora was still exploring the tree.

"That's Aurora," said Jake.

"Nice to meet you, Aurora," said Oliver, smiling.

"I'm Oliver and this is my friend—"

"Tom. Glad to meet you," interrupted Tom.

Aurora finally stepped back from the tree and took in the strangers. "Why are you dressed like that? And why are you wearing that hat?"

Tom and Oliver looked at their attire. "What do you mean, this is how we dress. What about you guys, why are you all wearing the same coloured clothes?"

"Are you armed?" asked Hayden, letting go of Crystal and clenching his fists by his side.

"Armed? No," replied Oliver. "Are you guys?" he asked.

Each member of the Cooinda group shook their heads.

Jake whispered into Aurora's ear, "We have to tell the authorities. They could be hostile."

"Why are you here?" asked Jake.

"It's a long story," replied Tom.

"Well start explaining," added Hayden, his fists still clenched.

There was laughter heard down the street.

"Quick! Someone is coming. You two hide behind the tree," instructed Aurora.

Tom and Oliver ran and hid behind the tree.

"What are we going to do with them?" mumbled Hayden.

"They can't stay here. We know nothing about them," said Jake.

"Where else are they going to go?" asked Aurora. She was apprehensive, but also curious to learn more about the strangers.

"Back where they came from," replied Jake.

Two young Cooinda citizens walked past the gardens laughing and shoving each other. Hayden, Crystal, Jake, and Aurora pretended to talk amongst themselves. Once the passers-by were no longer visible Aurora called for the boys to come out from behind the tree.

"Is there a key for that door?" asked Jake.

Oliver pulled out the electronic key from his pocket, that had allowed them entry into the passageway. "Only this," he said.

Jake took a few steps forward towards Oliver and Tom to glean a better look at the key. "Maybe it opens the doorway here?"

Jake walked past the boys and to the tree, looking for any signs of a way in opening the door.

"Can you see anything?" Aurora called.

"No," replied Jake. "It looks like a one-way entry."

"A one-way?" said Oliver. "That means we're stuck here?"

"Looks like it," said Jake, still inspecting the tree.

"I don't trust them," said Hayden.

Aurora attempted to pacify the group. "Everyone calm down. If they were here to hurt us, they would have done so by now."

Hayden brought his fists up to his face. "Yeah, well. I'm ready for them."

"Hayden," said Crystal, pulling on Hayden's suit.

"It's ok, babe. I'll protect you," added Hayden, through gritted teeth.

"Whoa. We're not here to hurt anyone," said Tom, taking a step forward towards the group. "We're as confused as you all are."

Jake returned to the group. "What do we do now then?"

"We hide them," said Aurora, taking a step towards the boys.

"Hide them? Aurora, we have to tell the authorities," Jake insisted.

"We don't want any trouble. Please don't hand us in, " pleaded Oliver.

"And why not?" added Hayden.

Aurora corralled Hayden, Crystal, and Jake together. "I don't think they're here to hurt us. I don't know how, but I think they somehow entered Cooinda by accident. Maybe we should try to find out? Maybe there is another world outside of here?"

"But we don't know anything about them, Aurora," said Jake. "What if they're infected with the phantom element?"

"Oh, I thought you said it was just a story?" Aurora replied.

"Phantom element," Hayden repeated. "Dad was right."

"Hang on a second. No one is saying it's real," said Aurora. "But maybe we should find out more about these guys? I say we vote. All in favour of handing them over to the authorities, raise your hand."

Jake and Hayden raised their hands.

"All those in favour of hiding them, raise your hand," said Aurora, raising her hand.

Crystal and Hayden raised their hands.

"You can't vote twice, Hayden," said Jake, pulling on Hayden's arm.

"Fine," huffed Hayden. "We'll hide them for now. But if they try to hurt any of us, I swear—"

"Ok. So where do hide them?" asked Aurora.

"They're sure as hell not staying with me," Jake asserted. "Hayden?"

"Don't look at me. There's barely enough room at my place as it is with Crystal and me."

"Well that leaves you, Aurora," said Crystal.

"No, no. I don't think that's a good idea," interjected Jake.

"You have any better idea?" replied Hayden.

"I can hide them," replied Aurora. "There's a spare room at my place. I can hide them there until we work out where we put them."

"Perfect," said Hayden, retreating from the group.

"Ok, guys. It's been decided. We won't hand you over to the authorities. We will hide you at Aurora's place for now."

"What are we going to do about their clothes?" asked Crystal.

The group pondered for a while, before Aurora remarked, "Jake lives nearby. He can grab some spares and race them back here."

Aurora watched Jake stomp his foot. "No way. I'm not lending them my clothes. I don't want them infected."

Hayden laughed. "Phantom element," he muttered.

"Fine. I'm the next closest. I guess I'll race back home and grab some of my dad's," replied Aurora. "I won't be too long."

"We'll stay here," said Hayden.

"I'll come with you," insisted Jake.

"Don't bother," replied Aurora. She was annoyed with Jake. She spun around and made foot towards the monorail station and boarded the monorail.

The trip back home raced by, much like the thoughts in her head. The monorail slowed into FAIRWEATHER, and Aurora leapt from the carriage, running full pelt back home.

"Hello, Aurora," chimed Nigel, the door slamming open by force from Aurora in her haste to locate her father's clothes.

"Aurora, is that you?" her mother could be heard saying from somewhere within the house.

"Yes, mum. I can't stay as I'm meeting with Jake," Aurora replied.

"What about our games night?" she called.

Aurora filtered out her mum as she was on a mission to find suitable clothes as quickly as possible and return to McPherson Gardens. She ransacked her parent's wardrobe and found two large grey casual suits. "This will have to do," Aurora said to herself. She swiped the clothes off their hangers, shoved them into a bag, and raced downstairs and out the door before her mum made any further comment. She scrambled back onto the monorail and made her way back towards the group. Racing up McPherson Parade, Jake called out upon seeing Aurora jogging towards the gardens. "What took you so long?"

The sky turned a deep blue.

"Sorry." She took the clothes out of her bag and handed them to Jake.

"Here, let me take them," said Jake.

"Where are they?" asked Aurora.

"Behind the tree," replied Jake, throwing the clothes around the trunk.

"Thanks," came a response from behind the tree.

The rest of the group anxiously waited for the boys to change.

"Come on guys," said Hayden, in haste.

The boys emerged from behind the tree.

"Great," said Jake. "So what do we do now?"

"We go with the plan of them going home with Aurora," replied Hayden. Now let's get out of this weird park," called Hayden.

"I think I should go with Aurora," said Jake.

"It'll be fine. I'll message you as soon as I get home, ok?" replied Aurora.

"Fine," said Jake.

"See you guys tomorrow," said Hayden. "I want to know all the goss."

As soon as they left McPherson Gardens, the group dispersed in all directions.

"Follow me," called Aurora to Oliver and Tom.

Oliver and Tom followed Aurora to the monorail station. Tom's mouth was wide open, like a Mongolian monk visiting a westernised city for the first time.

"Try to look inconspicuous, Oliver," Aurora remarked.

"This place is incredible!"

"Ok, stick close to me," said Aurora as she approached the

gate. Aurora presented her wrist to the gate sensor, activating the gate. Oliver was stuck to Aurora like a magnet.

"Phew, that was close," exhaled Aurora. "You can let go of me now, Oliver."

"Oh, sorry," replied Oliver. His cheeks reddened.

The monorail arrived and they promptly found a seat. There were not too many people on the carriage. The lady directly across from them tightened her gaze and openly displayed her suspicion of the trio. She fidgeted in her seat before disembarking the carriage, only to alight on the next.

Aurora whispered to Oliver and Tom, "Just don't say anything to anyone, ok? If anyone asks you a question, I will answer for you."

The boys nodded.

As the monorail headed towards the Source, Tom pointed. Aurora pulled on his arm. "And stop pointing."

"Sorry, Aurora. I'm trying," replied Tom. "What is that anyway?"

Aurora didn't respond.

The monorail came into Fairweather station.

"This is our stop. Let's go. Remember, follow me and don't point or say anything to anyone," Aurora said hurriedly.

They approached Aurora's house. "Right, hide around the side of the house while I make sure the house is clear."

"Got it," replied Oliver, grabbing Tom's arm.

"Hello, Aurora," chimed Nigel.

Aurora scampered into the house trying not to alert the household of her presence.

"Aurora! Is that you?" called her mum.

"Damn," Aurora muttered. "Yes, mum it's me," replied Aurora.

Her mother welcomed her into the lounge. "How was your time with Jake?"

"Ah, fine, thanks. Hey, I might head to bed, I'm really tired."

Her mum looked perplexed, "Everything alright, love?"

Aurora felt agitated, "Yeah, everything is fine, it's just been a big couple of days, that's all."

Her mum walked towards Aurora, "I think we might need to talk."

"Not now, mum. Can we maybe talk about it tomorrow?" Aurora said, combing her fingers through her hair.

"Sure. Go get some rest, and we will talk tomorrow," replied her mother, holding onto her daughter's hand.

Aurora gave her mother a peck on the cheek and walked upstairs towards her bedroom. Halfway up she turned back to check if her mother was still there. Content that the area was clear, Aurora tiptoed back down the stairs, towards the front door. She opened the door and poked her head around the corner.

"Oliver? Tom? Where are you?" she whispered.

Not a sound.

"Oliver? Tom?" she called again, this time with more inflection.

Still nothing.

Aurora wedged her foot against the door to keep it ajar whilst projecting her body further outside.

"Oliver! Tom!" she called again, almost certain that if they hadn't heard this time, the rest of the house surely had.

Oliver finally emerged from the side of the house.

"Oh, there you are," Oliver replied, with a sheepish grin on his face.

Aurora looked behind to see if anyone had heard her calls

before signalling them to come inside.

"Quick. Come in."

They leapt towards the entrance and peered into the house.

"Nice place," said Tom.

Aurora dragged Oliver and Tom inside and shoved them towards the spare room beside the kitchen. She could hear her mother rummaging around nearby.

Aurora pointed into the spare room and the boys crept in. Aurora quietly closed the door of the spare room behind her and whispered, "Stay here. I'll come back when everyone has gone to sleep."

Oliver nodded.

Aurora crept out of the room and tiptoed back to her room. Almost an hour passed before Aurora could no longer hear any sounds from downstairs. She gently opened the door and peered around the corner. The house was completely dark, apart from the Source's light streaming through the windows. She stepped down the stairway and towards the spare room. She didn't want to knock in case she awoke the household. Instead, she pushed on the door and found Oliver lying on the bed completely naked, apart from his underwear. Aurora blushed and hid behind her hands.

"Oh sorry," she whispered.

Oliver had his eyes closed but jolted upright upon hearing Aurora. "Oh, hi," he replied.

"Hi, Aurora," said Tom, sitting on the floor.

"Everything alright in here?" Aurora asked.

"Yep. It's just been a crazy day. Thanks for looking after us, by the way."

Aurora nodded, "Yeah, well, where else were you going to go? Sorry, we only have one bed."

"That's ok. He's used to lying on hard surfaces," smiled Oliver.

"I'm not sure your boyfriend was overly thrilled with this idea," said Tom, stretching his back.

"Who?" asked Aurora, with a puzzled expression.

"Jake, was it?" said Oliver.

"He's not my boyfriend, he's just a friend from work."

"If you say so," grinned Tom.

"We better get some rest," said Aurora. "We will work all this out tomorrow. Night."

"Night," said Oliver in Tom in unison.

Aurora crept out of the room and did a quick left and right before creeping up the stairs to her bedroom and sent Jake a message to say that the boys had settled in. She closed her eyes but was certain she was not going to get much sleep.

Chapter 16

Arnold Slater sat in silence in front of thirty-odd LED screens, housed on level three of the McPherson Building, opposite the McPherson Gardens. He enjoyed his job and was good at it. He had very little in the way of family, other than his lost brother, and his tomato bush, which he was so very fond of.

"Night, Mr Slater", announced Jerry, the cleaner, as he vacuumed past Arnold's doorway.

"Night, Jerry," replied Arnold, not bothering to look up from his work.

Arnold took a sip from his coffee cup. It had gone cold a long time ago. He took no notice and finished the remaining drink. He stood to fix himself another cup when he noticed activity on his screens.

"Whatever are they doing?" Arnold said to himself.

His pupils automatically dilated, taking in more of the scene.

"Are you almost done for the night, Mr Slater?" came a call from the other side of the room.

"Everything alright, Mr Slater?" came the call again. This time Arnold had heard.

"Huh? Ah, yes, thank you, Jerry. I'll just be—" Arnold's words faded out as he noticed the tree base opening.

"Alright, I'll see you tomorrow," said Jerry.

Arnold simply nodded.

He saw two men emerge from the tree. One wore a hat he had not seen since —

Arnold sat back in his chair and caressed the leaves of his beloved tomato bush, as he reflected on his past.

"Next," yelled a lady, holding an electronic tablet. "Please show me your lotto confirmation details."

Arnold showed the lady his confirmation letter from his phone.

"Thank you," replied the lady. "You won't be needing your hat though," she added.

Arnold removed his Akubra from his head and threw it onto the ground.

"Go on through," gestured the lady. "According to the instructions I have here, you won't require this drug."

Arnold fell off his chair, bringing him back to him witnessing the intruders. "Who are they talking to?" He adjusted the camera, however, the mechanism was stuck. "What's wrong with this stupid thing," Arnold cursed.

He ran towards the blinded window and opened the blinds. He now had a clear view of the gardens, with the tree in his central view. One of the members looked around, once in the direction of Arnold's window. Arnold ducked under the sill and counted to twenty, hoping it was enough not to be noticed.

He surreptitiously poked his head over the windowsill and noticed that the group had dispersed.

"Where did they go?" he mumbled to himself. He was annoyed with himself that he'd hidden so long, allowing them to escape.

He raced back to the screens to see if they appeared on any

of them. "It's like they vanished into thin air." He noticed movement on the screen that monitored the monorail station. He leaned forward, his nose almost touching the screen. "Is that—?" He activated the facial recognition and scanned the trio's faces. Only one of the faces was able to be identified; Aurora Jemmerson. Arnold reclined in his seat and tapped his fingers on the desk before he stood and made for the door. He ran down the stairs, often leaping three steps at a time. His chest tightened and he wheezed, but he was on a mission.

The basement level door flung open and impacted the polymer wall, giving a thud. He ran to the tree and found discarded clothes, including the Akubra hat. He bundled the clothes into his hands and raced back to his office. He threw the clothes into the bottom drawer of his desk and closed it shut. He ran to the men's bathroom and scrubbed his hands until they were almost raw. Looking up in the mirror, he saw an anguished-looking middle-aged man with beads of sweat on his forehead.

"What am I going to do?" he sighed. He strode back to his office and unlocked the lid on a red coloured, metal box, hidden in a bookcase. Inside was a phone. He picked it up and dialled 276653.

A voice answered on the other end, "Yes?"

"We have a problem."

Chapter 17

Aurora awoke from her vibrating wrist device. "It can't be time to wake up already," she said to herself. She silenced the device and rolled over.

"Aurora," her mum called. "Time to wake up."

"Got it," mumbled Aurora. She lay in bed thinking about her encounter with the strangers the previous night before she realised that they were hidden, in the spare room, downstairs.

She stumbled out of bed and fell onto the floor.

"Aurora, what's going on?" called her mother.

"Yes, mum," yelled Aurora, racing down the stairs.

"Morning, love," said Jasmine, as she pressed the button on the automated orange presser.

"Morning," replied Aurora.

"Everything alright?" asked her mother.

"Yeah, why wouldn't it be?"

"Just that your hand is shaking," replied Jasmine.

"Ah, yeah, I must have slept on it," said Aurora putting her hand behind her back.

"Well, I better go check to make sure your father is awake," said Jasmine who smiled at her daughter as she walked out of the room.

As soon as her mother left the kitchen, Aurora finished her

glass of orange juice and checked on Oliver. But not before she heard a sound in the backyard. *What was that?* She peered through the open door. She heard the noise again. She walked outside into her father's hydroponic vegetable garden.

"Hello," said a deep voice from behind her.

Aurora spun around, her pulse racing and her entire body tense. "Far out, Oliver. You scared me."

Oliver laughed. "Sorry, I couldn't resist. What are you doing out here anyway?"

"What are you doing out here?" insisted Aurora.

"I needed fresh air. The air down here is so much more refreshing than where we're from."

Aurora's hands were still shaking. "Is it? I need to talk to you and Tom about where you're from, actually. Where is Tom, anyway?"

"He's still in the room."

"Aurora," called her mum from inside the house.

"Shit. Hide in the garden shed. I'll come and find you soon."

"Ok."

"Coming," yelled Aurora as she rushed back inside and into the kitchen.

"What were you doing out there?"

"Out where? Oh, outside? Yes, I was watering the garden."

Jasmine poked her head forward. "You never water the garden, Aurora."

"Well now I have," replied Aurora giving a sheepish grin.

Jasmine looked at her wrist. "Goodness, you better hurry up. You have work, don't you?"

"Ah, yes. Ok. Good," said Aurora, frenziedly walking from the kitchen to her room.

Aurora showered and dressed and checked that the coast

was clear before stepping outside, to the garden shed.

"Ok, I have a plan. I'll sneak you into my work. I'll tell them you're on work experience."

Oliver nodded. "This will be cool," he replied excitedly.

"I'll check that it's clear. Get dressed and we'll get going."

"Can I have something to eat or drink at least?"

Aurora grunted, "I'll grab you a juice."

"Great. What about Tom?"

Aurora had momentarily forgotten about him. She phoned Jake from her ACCESS. "Hi Jake, it's me, Aurora."

"Hi, Aurora. How are you? How're the boys?"

"They're fine. I'm going to try and sneak them into the lab."

"Why?"

"They can't stay here. What if my parents find them?"

"Then they're not our problem. That's what."

"How could you be so inconsiderate, Jake?"

"Inconsiderate? Two complete strangers stumble into Cooinda and you think I'm inconsiderate?"

Aurora sensed Jake's agitation but was annoyed by his lack of compassion.

"Sorry, it's just—"

"Yeah, I know," said Aurora, looking Oliver up and down, while talking into her ACCESS. "I'll see you at the lab. We'll try to find out as much as we can about them."

"Ok, see you soon," replied Jake, hanging up the call.

"Stay behind me. I'll make sure we're clear," Aurora instructed Oliver.

Aurora scanned the garden and led Oliver to the house. She poked her head through the door. Content that there was no one nearby, they tiptoed to the spare room, where Tom was still asleep.

"Tom," said Oliver, attempting to rouse him.

"What, where am I?" asked Tom.

"That's a good question," replied Oliver, looking at Aurora. "Where are we?"

"Cooinda," replied Aurora. "It means, Happy Place."

"Cute," said Oliver. "Tom, we have to go."

"Go? Go where?"

"I'm going to sneak you two into the lab, where I work."

"Why?" asked Tom.

"You can't stay here. It's too risky," replied Aurora.

"Ugh. So much for my sleep in," said Tom, getting to his feet.

"I'll leave you boys to get ready. I'll come back in a few minutes."

Both Tom and Oliver nodded. Aurora sneaked out of the spare room and prepared two orange juices for the boys. Juices in hand, she whispered, "Are you ready?" through the door.

"Yes," replied Oliver.

Aurora opened the door and was met by Oliver and Tom, dressed in their new attire.

"Right let's go," instructed Aurora. She checked the lounge room and waved for them to follow her.

They left the house and walked to the station and waited for the monorail.

"Ok, leave the talking to me," instructed Aurora.

"Got it," replied Oliver.

The monorail approached the station. They embarked on the carriage and sat in silence for the short journey to Source Square.

They disembarked the monorail and walked through the centre of the square, past the Source.

"Is that what we saw last night?" asked Oliver.

"Yes, it's called the Source," replied Aurora.

"The Source? What is it?" asked Tom.

"It provides light, energy, water, air, you name it," replied Aurora.

"It does all that?" said Oliver, in awe.

"The lab is this way. Follow me."

Aurora led Oliver and Tom to the laboratory. At the entry, she got the attention of a security robot.

"Hello, I have two work experience students here that will be working with me for a little bit."

"Identify yourself," replied the robot.

Aurora pressed her ACCESS onto the robot's sensor.

"Welcome Aurora. Authorisation required for your request," the guard instructed.

"Authorisation?"

"Authorisation approved," called Jake, who swiped his AC-CESS across the guard's scanner.

"Access granted," replied the bot.

"Thanks, Jake," said Aurora.

Jake smiled. "No problem."

Oliver and Tom followed Aurora and Jake through the gates and into their laboratory.

"Don't touch anything," said Aurora handing Oliver and Tom a lab coat each.

"Why do I need to wear this then?" asked Oliver.

"So that you fit in," said Jake.

"Oliver, you can sit with me. Tom, you go with Jake," Aurora directed.

Hayden and Crystal strolled into the room.

"Hi, guys," smiled Hayden. "How did you two sleep?" he said, looking at Oliver and Tom.

"Fine," they replied.

"Why are you here, Hayden?" Aurora asked.

"Someone's a bit jumpy this morning," replied Hayden. "Don't forget, my vote ensured they weren't handed over to the authorities."

Aurora disliked Hayden's smugness. But she also knew she had to try and get along with him, for the time being.

Hayden and Crystal grabbed a chair and sat beside Oliver and Tom.

"Who's going to start then?" asked Hayden, looking at Oliver and Tom.

"I will," replied Oliver. "What do you want to know?"

"Let's start from the beginning," prompted Aurora.

"Ok, well, as you know, I'm Oliver and this is Tom."

"This could be a long story," sighed Hayden.

"We were on an expedition, collecting rocks, bones, and fossils," Oliver, continued.

"Fossils?" inquired Jake.

"Yeah, like plants and animals stuck in rock," Tom, interrupted.

Oliver shook his head, "Anyway, our 4WD broke down."

"4WD?" asked Jake.

"Jake, if you keep interrupting, we will never hear their story," replied Hayden.

"Sorry," said Jake. "Continue."

"We broke down and we walked to this old, abandoned house."

"It was creepy," added Tom.

"All we found was a passageway. We then hitched a ride into town and stayed at a hotel."

"A ho—" Jake started saying.

Hayden shook his finger at Jake.

"Anyway, Mike takes us to our 4WD, but then leaves us. We head back to the house and heard a noise," continues, Oliver.

"What sort of noise? asked Aurora. She was intrigued by the story.

"Like this," said Oliver, knocking his fist against the bench.

"That was me!" exclaimed Aurora. "We heard knocking on our end too."

"Really?" Oliver replied.

"Then what happened?" Hayden prompted.

"Well, then the passageway wall opened."

"That was a bit of an anticlimax," Hayden replied.

"Ok, that explains how you got here. Tell us about your world," said Aurora, sitting on the edge of her seat.

"It's nothing like this," snorted Tom. "There's a lot more dirt."

"What about the phantom element?" Aurora asked.

"Now we're talking," said Hayden, flinging his arm over the seat.

"Phantom element?" quizzed Oliver.

"There's a story about this mystical and invisible entity that causes disease," replied Aurora. "Apparently that's why all of us are down here. To escape this thing."

"Hang on a second," said Tom. "You're telling me that a whole heap of you were from where we're from, and you left us?"

"I wouldn't put it like that," replied Jake.

"You don't suppose they're talking about the NIFA virus do you?" said Tom, to Oliver.

"NIFA virus?" said Crystal.

"Yeah, about ten years ago there was a really bad virus that went around the earth. It was a mutated virus. A combination of two deadly viruses. People were dying by the thousands every minute around the globe. It lasted for years."

Aurora gasped, "That sounds terrible." Aurora was despondent. She hated seeing people suffer.

"It was," added Tom. "We had to wear these uncomfortable masks wherever we went. It was our only protection."

"Masks?" Aurora asked.

"Yeah. Actually, I might have a photo of me wearing one," said Oliver, pulling his phone from his pocket. "Damn, battery's flat."

"I have a feeling I know what masks you're talking about," said Aurora.

"Is the virus still around?" asked Jake.

"Only in small areas," replied Oliver. "It's no longer a pandemic."

"See, I was right," gloated Hayden.

Aurora combed her fingers through her hair. She was amazed that there was another world outside of Cooinda and she was keen to learn more.

"Do you guys maybe want to come around to our place tonight for a celebration dinner?" asked Hayden to Oliver and Tom.

"Ah, I'm not sure," replied Oliver.

"I'm keen," smiled Tom.

"I don't know, Tom, we've only been here for less than twenty-four hours."

"Come on, it'll be fun," insisted Tom.

"No," replied Oliver.

"Fine," remarked Tom. "I'll go on my own."

"We can drop him back home later tonight if you like?" said Crystal.

"I don't think it's a good idea," Aurora replied.

"Please," pleaded Tom. "It'll only be for an hour or so."

"Yeah, it's nothing huge," added Crystal.

Aurora was suspicious but conceded. *Maybe this might allow me time to get to know Oliver a little better,* she said to herself. "Fine, I'll send you my address. You can drop him over later tonight. Looks like I'm introducing you to my parents, Oliver."

"Do you think that's a good idea?" said Jake, sitting upright on his seat.

"I hate sneaking around all the time," Aurora replied.

Hayden stood, "I'll come by later this afternoon, Tom. Enjoy the rest of your day, guys. Come on Crystal."

Hayden and Crystal left the laboratory, leaving Oliver, Tom, Jake, and Crystal to converse.

"Can I ask you guys something?" Oliver asked the group. "If you all escaped, how come none of you have any recollection?"

"I've wondered that myself," replied Aurora. "I don't know."

"And how did you all escape without anyone knowing?" added Tom.

"That, I also don't know," replied Aurora. She was annoyed that she didn't know the answers to these questions. *Maybe mum might know* she thought to herself.

Chapter 18

Jasmine was in her kitchen preparing a vegetable frittata for dinner when she heard a knock at the door. She paused the 3D printer and walked to the front door. Upon opening she was faced with a tall man, with broad shoulders, wearing a black cloak. Jasmine's throat closed. *No, it can't be* she thought to herself.

"Jasmine Jemmerson?" inquired Arnold.

"Ah, yes, that's me," replied Jasmine.

"I'm detective Arnold Slater from the Cooinda Police Department."

"Oh, yes, Detective Slater."

"Can I come in?"

"Ah, well." Jasmine looked back into the house. "I don't think that's possible right now."

Arnold attempted to peek in through the doorway. "Very well."

"Perhaps I can visit you at the station?"

Arnold loosened his suit from around his neck. "Ah, no I don't think that'll be necessary Mrs Jemmerson. Is Barry home?" Arnold fumbled. "Ah, Mr Jemmerson, that is."

Jasmine's hands began to shake which Arnold noticed. "Ah, no, he is not here at the moment."

"Jazz," called Barry from inside the house. "Who's at the door?"

"No one, dear," replied Jasmine.

"Everything ok, Mrs Jemmerson?" asked Arnold.

"Yes of course. You've just caught me at a bad time, that's all."

"I see."

Barry appeared at the door. "Hello there," he said.

"Hello Mr Jemmerson," replied Arnold.

"Who are you?" asked Barry.

"Oh, sorry, yes, I'm Detective Arnold Slater."

"Glad to meet you, Detective. Is something wrong?"

"Not exactly."

Barry looked puzzled. "Ok, so why are you here?"

"I'm doing a routine neighbourhood check. That's all."

"Oh, I see. Jasmine was telling me there was a report of a disturbance the other night," replied Barry.

No one said anything for a few seconds before Arnold finally said, "Well, everything seems to be in order here. Thank you for your time Mr and Mrs Jemmerson."

"How do you know our names?" asked Barry.

"I'm a detective. It's my job to know," replied Arnold who gave a nod and walked back towards his car. He paused and turned towards Jasmine and Barry, who were both still standing in the doorway. "Oh, I almost forgot. Is your daughter home?

"Aurora? Why?" asked Jasmine.

"I've been informed that she's won a scientific prize. I wanted to congratulate her myself," grinned Arnold.

"She's not here," Jasmine replied.

"I see. Perhaps another time then."

Arnold turned and walked to his car.

"Strange man," said Barry, as he closed the door.

"I'm going to lie down for a bit," said Barry.

"Sure, dear," replied Jasmine. She sat on the couch and buried her face in her hands and began to sob. She was not ready to face her past so soon.

Jasmine thought back to her time at university.

"I think Jasmine might win," whispered Bernadette Hisplop to Barry Jemmerson, who were both watching the final of a chess tournament, held in the lobby of the Storey Building.

"Who's her opponent?" asked Barry.

"Arnold is his name. He's a bit of a weird guy," replied Bernadette.

"Weird? In what way?"

"A friend of mine says she sees him just staring up at the sky all the time. He has no friends. He counts the number of steps to each lecture hall. Apparently, if he lands on an odd number, he'll take another step."

"We all have our quirks," smiled Barry. "I hope Jasmine wins. I promised her I would take her to *Try Thai* for dinner if she won. She loves that place. I don't mind it either, to be fair. The Chicken Cashew is my favourite."

"She's lucky to have to you, Barry."

"Guys, I'm trying to concentrate," exclaimed Jasmine.

"Oh sorry, Jazz. I didn't think you could hear us," said Barry.

"It's your turn," insisted Arnold.

Jasmine examined the chessboard. She had memorised and used many of the best-known moves, such as the Benko Gambit, Alekhine's Defence, and Albin's Counter gambit, but none of them had forced a check-mate. She noticed a mark on Arnold's left wrist. He quickly retracted his hand when he noticed her looking at it.

"Do you want me to make a move instead?" asked Arnold, touching Jasmine's leg under the table.

Jasmine felt uncomfortable and moved her leg away from his hand. She cornered his king with her bishop and rook. She looked at Arnold's face. His smirk changed to the look of frustration. He stood and raced out of the hall, holding his stomach.

"What's going on?" asked Jasmine.

"He has irritable bowel," replied Bernadette.

"How would you know that?" asked Barry.

"My friend said she sees him run out of the lectures all the time. He told the class that he has gut issues."

"Congratulations, Miss Spencer," announced the Master of Ceremonies. "You have been won the annual University Chess Championship."

Some months later, Arnold came across Jasmine's path on his way to his accounting lecture.

"Hello, Jasmine," called Arnold, staring at her breasts.

"Ah, hi," she replied, clasping her stethoscope in her hand.

"Where are you off to?"

"I've got a physical examination lecture today."

"Maybe I can be your patient," smiled Arnold.

"Ah, I think they've already been assigned." Jasmine looked for an escape. "Anyway, I have to get going."

"Oh, sure thing. I'll maybe see you around."

Jasmine strutted to her lecture, without looking back.

A few weeks later, she received a gift, in her post box. She opened the gift and inside was a note that read,

Dear Jasmine,

I have hand-carved a chess piece for you. I enjoyed our game of chess together. Hopefully, we can play more together.
Yours always
AS

"What is it with this guy?" snarled Jasmine, throwing the chess piece into the bin.

"Hi, sweetie," said Barry, giving her a passionate kiss on the lips. "Everything alright?"

Jasmine smiled at Barry, "Yes, it is now. You ready to go see that movie?"

"Yep, let's go."

Barry and Jasmine walked across the university square, holding hands. Later that night, walking back to their dormitories, they heard a sound in the bushes.

"Stay close," insisted Barry, pulling Jasmine behind him.

Jasmine's heart raced. "Who's there?" She saw a figure retreat into the darkness.

"What the heck was that?" asked Barry.

Jasmine's face screwed up, furious that her privacy had been invaded. "I have an idea."

"Hey, I'm going to grab some beers, do you want to come?" asked Barry.

"No, I've got some study to do. I'll see you tomorrow," she replied, giving Barry a peck on the cheek.

"Ok."

A few hours later, Jasmine received news that Barry had been in an accident. She raced to the hospital and wept uncontrollably upon seeing Barry hooked up to tubes strewn across his body.

"Barry, are you ok?" cried Jasmine.

Barry groaned. "Yeah, I'm ok, Jazz. They said I was in an accident?"

Jasmine looked towards one of the nursing staff, visibly concerned with his retrograde amnesia.

The nurse simply smiled and walked out of the room.

"What happened, Jazz?" inquired Barry.

"I'm not sure, but right now, you need to look after yourself."

"Here. I got something for you," said Jasmine, placing a tomato bush on the bedside table.

"Oh, thank you," smiled Barry. "Solanum lycopersicum."

"If you say so."

"The police said my brakes were tampered with."

Jasmine expressed concern. "Tampered with? Someone deliberately did this to you?"

Barry had a coughing fit, prompting Jasmine to fetch a glass of water. "Here," she said, holding the glass to Barry's mouth.

"Thanks."

"Who would do such a thing?" Jasmine was now angry.

After several hours of comforting Barry, she returned to campus by bus. She had only disembarked the bus when Arnold emerged from the dark.

"Oh my God. Arnold. You scared the crap out of me," exclaimed Jasmine.

"Where have you been, Jasmine?"

Jasmine's stomach turned. That uneasy feeling returned. "At the hospital. A friend of mine was hurt."

"Well, you won't need to worry about him now that he is out of the picture" replied Arnold.

"Wait, hang on. You did this? You hurt Barry?"

Arnold smiled and, after an awkward pause replied, "Surely you realise that you and I are meant to be together, Jasmine?"

He reached out his hand in an attempt to console Jasmine.

"How could you? What a terrible person you are," she yelled. "He's still alive you know!"

Jasmine ran towards the dormitory, with Arnold in pursuit. She stopped in her tracks.

"Stay away from me, you hear? I don't want to ever see you again. You're a psychopath, Arnold, who has no friends, no feelings for other people, and a dodgy stomach." She ran to her room as fast as she could, without looking back.

Jasmine's mind returned to her sitting on the couch in her lounge room. She wiped the tears from her eyes.

Chapter 19

Aurora led Oliver down Princeton Street, towards her home. "Let me do the talking, ok?"

"Sure."

Aurora closed her eyes, willing the door to open.

"Hello, Aurora," Nigel announced.

"Wow, that is awesome. How did you do that?" asked Oliver.

"Do what?"

"Open the door."

"Using my mind. Do you not have that where you're from?"

"I wish. The closest we have to that are magicians claiming they're able to guess what word someone from the audience is thinking about."

Aurora walked into the lounge room with Oliver remaining outside.

"Mum," Aurora called.

Jasmine walked down the stairs and embraced her daughter. "Aurora, I'm so happy to see you."

"I'm happy to see you too, mum," replied Aurora, baffled by her mum's exuberance.

Aurora wrangled out of her mother's embrace. "Mum, I need to talk to you."

"Yes, I need to talk to you too."

"There's a work experience person that wants me to go over some of my work."

"Oh, ok. Are you going back to the lab?"

"No, actually I was wondering if he could maybe come here?"

Jasmine swallowed hard. "He?"

"Ah, yes. His name is Oliver."

Oliver appeared at the doorway. "Hello."

"Oh, hello," replied Jasmine surprised by his appearance. "Well, I guess that's fine. Would you like to come in Oliver? You can call me Jasmine."

"Yes, thank you," said Oliver.

Oliver walked into the lounge, where all awkwardly stood for some time.

"Would you like to stay for dinner?" asked Jasmine.

"Yes, that would be lovely, thank you," replied Oliver.

"Great. I'll be back shortly," said Jasmine, who walked into the kitchen.

"Just sit and eat your meal ok?" whispered Aurora to Oliver.

"Yeah, yeah. It'll be fine, Aurora. Don't stress," replied Oliver.

"Do you like frittata, Oliver?" called Jasmine from the kitchen.

"Ah, yes thank you," replied Oliver.

"Ok, dinner is ready. I'll go and find Barry," said Jasmine.

Aurora and Oliver walked into the kitchen and sat down at the table.

"Barry, this is Aurora's work experience student, Oliver," introduced Jasmine.

"Glad to meet you, Oliver. Barry's my name," said Barry who took a seat at the table, opposite Oliver and Aurora.

"Hello, Barry," replied Oliver.

Jasmine took her seat. "Everyone help yourselves."

Aurora inspected the garden salad, boiled potatoes, and the frittata before asking Oliver, "What would you like?"

"I'm not fussy."

"Do you want me to serve for you?" asked Aurora.

"Aurora, I'm sure he's more than capable," grinned Jasmine.

Oliver used the tongs and took a dozen leaves of the salad and placed them onto his plate.

"How are you enjoying the lab?" asked Jasmine to Oliver.

"Yes, it's great thanks. I'm learning a lot," replied Oliver.

"What was your specialty at university, Oliver?" asked Jasmine.

Oliver covered his mouth as he attempted to answer with a mouthful of food. "Ah, arch—" He stopped short of finishing his sentence. "Archaeorobotics," he replied.

"What's that?" asked Barry who took a bite of his food.

"Oh, it's a new area," replied Oliver.

There was a knock at the door. Jasmine stood from the table and answered the door. "Aurora, Jake is here," she called from the front entrance.

Aurora stopped eating. "What's Jake doing here?" She stood and welcomed Jake at the door.

"Hi, Aurora, " greeted Jake.

"Hi, what are you doing here?"

"Can I come in?"

"Ah, we're just in the middle of—"

"Hello, Jake," said Jasmine, who appeared at the door.

"Oh, hello Mrs Jemmerson."

"Jasmine, remember?"

"Oh, yes, sorry."

"Would you like to come in for dinner? Aurora's new work experience student is here too. Have you met him?"

"Ah, yes I have. He was at the lab today. That's ok. I'll catch up with Aurora tomorrow."

"Don't be silly. Come on in. This way I can keep an eye on Aurora," laughed Jasmine.

"Oh, ok then," replied Jake.

Aurora let Jake in and led him through to the kitchen.

"Take a seat, Jake," said Barry pointing to an empty chair, at the end of the table.

"Help yourself," said Jasmine. "Oliver was just telling us about his studies. What was the name of that topic again?"

Oliver had a mouthful of food again.

"Mum, let him eat," said Aurora.

"How was the festival the other night, Jake?" asked Jasmine turning her attention to Jake.

"Ah, it was fine," replied Jake, who looked over to Aurora.

"So whereabouts are you from Oliver?" asked Barry.

"Quilpie," replied Jake.

"Quilpie?" returned Jasmine.

"Never heard of it," mumbled Barry.

Jasmine dropped her fork and shakily picked up her glass of water.

"Why's your hand shaking, Jazz?" asked Barry.

Jasmine studied Oliver. "So who's your favourite band, Oliver?"

"Band?" replied Oliver who began to sweat.

"Mum," exclaimed Aurora.

"Menace, isn't it Oliver?" Jake interjected.

"I was asking Oliver," Jasmine replied, sternly.

"Ah, yes it's Menace," said Oliver.

"What do you think of our Mayor, Oliver?" insisted Jasmine.

Oliver looked at Aurora and Jake for reassurance.

"Mum," exclaimed Aurora.

"No, I want to hear Oliver's opinion on this," said Jasmine, who leaned forward.

"Well, ah, I think he's very nice," replied Oliver.

"He? Our Mayor is a she," said Jasmine who grasped her hand around her knife.

"Oh, yes, I meant she," stammered Oliver.

Aurora's wrist device vibrated. It was a message.

Hello, You'd best come to the McPherson Building, Level 3 Room 121 now if you want to see your new friend alive. Bring the other one too. A.

Chapter 20

An hour earlier back at the laboratory...

Crystal walked into the laboratory and found Tom, sitting beside Jake, by the bio-hazard cabinet. "Hey, Tom."

"Oh, hi," replied Tom, his bored expression was replaced with excitement.

"You ready to go?"

"I sure am. Sorry, Jake, I have to get going. It's been great watching you all day."

Jake turned and faced Crystal, "He's all yours."

Jake hung up his lab coat and waved to Oliver. "See ya later, mate. You'll regret not coming."

"Have him back by seven," Aurora demanded to Crystal.

"Sure thing," replied Crystal.

Crystal escorted Tom out of the laboratory and walked to Source Square, to board the monorail.

"Why are we walking?" asked Tom. "I assumed Hayden was driving us to his place?"

"He'll join us later," replied Crystal. "He's busy with work at the moment. We can still have fun though," she added, giving a gentle squeeze of Tom's buttocks.

Tom was surprised by Crystal's flirtatiousness but enjoyed

it.

They boarded the monorail and travelled to Grayston Station.

"This is our stop," said Crystal, alighting from the monorail.

Tom followed Crystal's lead to Hayden's apartment.

"Hello, Crystal," chimed Nigel.

"That's incredible," said Tom, seeing the door open. "That's a neat party trick."

"Come on in," said Crystal, waving Tom into the tiny apartment.

"Nice place," Tom remarked. He noticed a machine sitting on the lounge room coffee table. "Wow, what's this?" he said. He pressed the touch screen and the machine came to life.

"Hello, how can I help you?" said the machine.

"Whoa!"

The screen provided options to choose from. *'Make bed'*, *'Turn on TV'*, *'Turn on shower'*

"What is this thing?"

"It's called Automate," Crystal replied, walking to the machine. "It practically does everything."

"This must have cost a fortune?"

"Cost?"

"Yeah, you know? Money?"

"I haven't heard of that."

"You don't have money here?"

"No, I don't think so."

Tom was intrigued. "You mean to say, all of this is free?" he said, looking around the room.

"Yeah, the government gives it to us. We just have to work and we get time credits to talk to the Divine."

"The Divine? What the hell is that?"

"It's our source of knowledge."

"You get to work for free? I'm really starting to like this place."

Crystal smiled. "What say I grab us a drink. Home-made lemonade?"

"Sounds good," replied Tom, reclining in the sofa chair.

"Make yourself comfortable, I'll be back in a minute." Crystal walked from the lounge into the kitchen and prepared the drinks.

"So what do you do at the lab?" Tom called, from the lounge room.

"I work in the artificial intelligence section," she replied.

"Artificial intelligence? That sounds fancy."

"Do you not have that where you're from?"

"Are you kidding? We've been stuck in the stone age for the last decade, thanks to NIFA."

Crystal returned to the lounge room, carrying two glasses of lemonade. "Here, this is yours," she said, handing a glass to Tom.

"Thanks."

"Sounds like that virus did a lot of damage?"

"Yeah, sure did," he replied, taking a sip from his drink. "Oh, wow. This is fantastic. I can really taste the lemons. Very refreshing."

"Thank you. So what are your plans?"

"Plans?"

"Yeah, I mean, are you planning on going back?"

"I have no idea. It looks like it was a one-way entry, so you might be stuck with me here," he smiled. "Maybe you can show me around the city?"

"Sure. It won't take long to see," she smiled.

"Is it a big city?"

Alana shook her head. "No, I think it's about ten square kilometres."

Tom computed before replying, "Ah, right." Tom rubbed his temples.

"You ok?" asked Crystal.

"Ah, yeah. I just feel a bit weird," Tom replied, his head bobbing.

"Just relax, Tom."

"What's going on?" exclaimed Tom.

"You'll be fine. I just put a little Salvia in your drink. It'll make you relax."

Tom collapsed in a heap on the floor. His eyes were fixed and dilated.

There was a knock at the door. She opened it and was met by Arnold.

"Is he out?" Arnold asked.

Crystal nodded.

"Right, I'll grab him," said Arnold who walked in and grabbed Tom's body and threw it over his shoulder. "Gee, he's not light," he exclaimed. He carried Tom out of the apartment and sat him in the backseat of his car. "You sit with him in the back," he instructed Crystal.

The car drove off towards the McPherson Building.

Chapter 21

Aurora covered her wrist and looked at Oliver. "We need to go," she said anxiously.

"I think you need to tell us who you are and where you're from, Oliver," insisted Jasmine, pounding her fist on the table.

"Huh?" said Oliver.

"You know exactly what I mean. I knew something wasn't right when I saw your complexion."

Oliver inspected his skin.

"The freckles. No one here has freckles," she said wielding her knife at Oliver. "The Source doesn't emit ultraviolet rays as the sun does."

Oliver stood up from the table.

"What are you talking about mum?" Aurora added, standing beside Oliver.

"Ok, everyone just needs to calm down," said Barry.

"He's an intruder. He's not from here, are you Oliver?" said Jasmine, pointedly.

"But, how?" muttered Aurora to her mother.

"Not everyone's memory was erased," replied Jasmine who stood and walked towards Oliver still wielding the knife, forcing Oliver to retreat into the lounge room.

Everyone followed.

Aurora ran and stood between Oliver and her mother, to act as a shield. "Mum put the knife down. What are you doing?" She was terrified by her mother's rage.

"We know nothing about him," asserted Jasmine. "We were fortunate to be brought here to protect us from people like him. How did you get here?" she demanded.

"Mum, he and Tom have told us all of this," replied Aurora.

"Tom? There's more of you," grunted Jasmine, taking a step towards Aurora and Oliver.

Jake stepped into the scene. "Jasmine, I know this is all a surprise. Trust me, it was a surprise for us too. In fact, I wanted to hand them over to the authorities, but your daughter convinced me not to."

Jasmine lowered the knife but kept her focus on Oliver. "Are you ill? Aurora, get away from him, he might be sick."

"Jasmine, it's ok. I'm not sick," replied Oliver, raising his arms in surrender.

Barry took hold of Jasmine's hand and clutched the knife from her. "It's ok, dear. Maybe we should hear him out."

"Dad, that sounds like a fantastic idea, but right now we have to rescue Tom," said Aurora. She was anxious to leave to aid Tom.

"Rescue him?" replied Oliver.

"I received a message just now. Tom's in trouble," replied Aurora. "Mum, we need to go to the McPherson Building. Now! Oliver can explain everything on the way. And you can explain to us how you knew and how we got here."

"I'll drive, but there's not enough room for everyone," exclaimed Barry.

"I'll go back home. Let me know what happens," replied Jake.

"We'll be back shortly," said Aurora.

The group managed to squeeze into the small Gemetra and drove hastily to the McPherson building.

Chapter 22

In Quilpie, Mike received a phone call from the local police.

"Morning, Mike, It's Detective Cooper here. Can I come and say hello to you in about half an hour?"

"Sure, Bill," replied Mike. "Everything alright?"

"Yeah, yeah, just chasing up some leads on a missing person. Two missing persons, actually. I'll see you at the Dirt Cafe?"

"Sure thing. See you then."

Mike was slightly anxious, particularly when hearing about the missing persons. *Surely it can't be those two boys I dropped off?* He resumed manicuring the hedge outside the hotel.

A half-hour later, Mike pulled up outside the Dirt Café. He noticed the police car. He went inside, where the waitress welcomed him.

"Good morning, Mike."

"Morning, Betty. Bill here?"

"Yep, he's just over there," replied Betty, pointing in the direction of where Bill was seated.

Mike approached the table.

"Morning, Bill."

"Oh, hi there Mike. Take a seat, mate."

Betty quickly presented the menu to Mike. "Would you like to start with any drinks, Mike?"

"Just the usual, thanks, Betty."

"Sure thing." Betty smiled proceeded to the kitchen.

"So, how you been, Mike? Been busy?" asked Bill.

"Yeah, it has been busy. Mainly with the hotel, though. Not much work with the service station."

Bill smiled and took another sip of his coffee. "So you're probably wondering why I called you in, hey?"

Mike fingered the dog-eared the menu. "Yeah, I guess."

Bill looked around the café and drew closer to Mike. "Listen, there's goss that there might be two guys missing and you might know something about it?"

Mike looked towards Betty preparing his tomato juice, then back to Mike. "Do I need a lawyer, Bill?"

Bill laughed. "Only if you killed them, mate. Just tell me what you know."

Betty approached the table with Mike's drink.

"You know what you might like to eat, Mike?" Betty asked.

Mike scanned the menu without paying much attention. "I'll just have the poached eggs thanks, Betty," replied Mike.

"Ok, sure thing."

"Look," started Mike. "They were staying at the hotel and I was asked to drop them back to their vehicle, which was broken down out of town. So I drove them out, fixed their 4WD, and we said our goodbyes.

Bill Cooper had been a detective with the Quilpie police force for over fifteen years and knew everyone in the town, along with their mannerisms. He had a knack for picking up on whether people were telling the truth or not, and Mike's story, along with his mannerism of pulling on his eyebrows; four times on each side, raised suspicion.

"So what was wrong with their 4WD, Mike?"

"Ah, the fan belt. It needed a new fan belt. Luckily, I had a spare one with me. Right as rain now, it is," replied Mike with a forced grin.

"Where exactly was the vehicle, Mike?"

Mike began to feel several beads of sweat forming on his brow and fanned himself. "Geez, it's warm here today, isn't it?"

"Mike? The 4WD. Where was the 4WD?" insisted Bill.

"A little past that house."

"What house?"

Mike's eggs arrived at the table.

"You want any salt and pepper, Mike?" asked Betty.

Mike waved Betty off. "No thanks, Betty. That's fine."

"You know," replied Mike nodding his head in its direction. "The creepy house."

Bill sat back in his seat and sighed. "Oh, Mike, that house is just old, that's all. It's been left abandoned for years. Ever since—" Bill's voice faded as he looked out the window.

"Ever since what?" prompted Mike.

"It was a long time ago. I was a young constable at the time. Pete was his name." Bill smiled.

"Pete?" inquired Mike.

"Yeah, he owned the house, along with his wife Rebecca. Bloody hell, Rebecca. She was some oil painting." Bill's eyes lit up.

"Was she?" said Mike cutting his toast into small-sized bits.

"From memory, I think she used to make cakes and scones for the Country Women's Association. They had two little rascals, always up to no good."

"Aren't all kids?" replied Mike.

"Yeah, I guess you're right. Anyway, we got a call one night.

There were reports of gunshots at the property. So we drove there and we saw poor old Pete and his beautiful wife dead on the floor."

"Mike stopped chewing. "God, that sounds terrible."

Bill rubbed his neck. "Yeah, it was. There was blood everywhere. I can still smell it, you know? That'll never leave me I don't reckon."

"What happened?" asked Mike.

"Murder, suicide," said Bill who gave his cup a swirl. "Bloody kids were a mess. They sat there stunned as mullets. Must have been terrible for them."

"Far out," replied Mike. "What happened to them?"

Bill shook his head. "Don't know. Some uncle took them under his wing I think." He gulped the rest of his coffee. "Betty, can I get a refill please?"

"Sure thing, Bill," replied Betty from the kitchen.

"I've heard that people have seen ghosts walking alongside the road, outside the property. Scares the crap out of me," Mike added, giving a shiver.

Bill shrugged, "You going to eat your food?"

Mike poked his eggs, releasing their yolks. He was no longer hungry. "Look, I dropped them off at their 4WD. I had a look under the bonnet and told them I needed to go back into town to fetch a fan belt."

"So you didn't fix their car?" pressed Bill.

"No. I was going to come back. I promise," implored Mike.

"So you left them out there?" asked Bill.

"Only for a bit. I was going to go back out there and fix their ride." Mike looked up towards Bill, who was looking directly at him.

"Why didn't you go back?"

"I got distracted."

"Distracted? With what in particular?"

"Work."

Bill groaned. "Can anyone confirm your whereabouts at the time, Mike?"

"Yeah, Di."

"How is your Mrs these days?"

"She's not my Mrs, Bill. She's just— a convenience."

"Can I have any of that?" asked Bill, pointing to Mike's uneaten food.

"Sure."

Bill ripped off a piece of Mike's toast and threw it into his mouth.

"So what do we do now?" asked Mike.

"*We* don't do anything. You have already done enough damage, Mike. Now I will have to find them." Bill rubbed his hands over his aged face. "We will head out to the house first thing tomorrow. In the meantime, don't leave town, you hear me, Mike?"

"Loud and clear, Bill. But I don't think you'll find them at the house."

"Why so?"

"One of the boy's said to me that he hated the house. I doubt they'd go there."

"Fair enough. All the same, I think we'll just cover all bases."

Bill stood up from the table. "Don't worry about the coffee, Betty. I've got work to do."

"Ok, sure thing Bill," replied Betty. "It's on the house today, by the way."

"Thanks, Betty," Bill winked to Betty.

Bill left the café, leaving Mike behind with his half-eaten

breakfast. Except, he was no longer hungry, and was beginning to feel a little queasy in the stomach.

Chapter 23

Barry brought the car to an abrupt stop outside the McPherson building. They hustled out of the car and ran to the door located on the ground floor. Aurora grabbed the handle.

"Wait. What if it's a trap?" said Jake.

"We have no choice, Jake. If we don't go in, Tom will be killed."

"We all could be killed," he replied.

"Come on, Aurora. Open the door!" exclaimed Oliver.

Aurora looked at Jake with sullen eyes before turning the handle. They raced up the stairwell and surged into the hallway on level three.

"Quick, we need to find room one-two-one," Aurora insisted

"Here it is," announced Jasmine.

They heard noises inside.

"They will be here any minute now. It's your move," said a male voice.

"That sounds like Arnold's," Jasmine remarked. She pounded on the door. The footsteps were heard approaching the door before it opened.

"Jasmine. What brings you here?" inquired Arnold.

"You know this man?" Aurora asked her mother, with surprise.

"Unfortunately," she replied, "We go back a long way."

"Seems we keep running into each other, don't we?" said Arnold to Aurora. He towered over her.

"What do you want from us?" Aurora screamed. She was on the verge of breaking down.

"He doesn't want you, dear. He wants me," Jasmine replied, looking intently at Arnold. Let them go, Arnold. This is between you and me."

Arnold howled. "Unfortunately, it has now become a great deal more complicated."

"Oliver! Is that you?" called Tom from within the room, almost in hysterics.

Oliver stepped forward and put his hand on the door. "Let him go."

"Ah, what do we have here?" smirked Arnold.

"We'll get you out of here, mate. Just sit tight," yelled Oliver.

Arnold laughed. "He's sitting tight, alright." He opened the door fully for all to see Tom bounded to a chair seated at a chess table.

"You're a psychopath, Arnold. You always have been and you always will be," exclaimed Jasmine.

Arnold looked confused. "How could you remember any of the past?"

"I must have a genetic mutation. The drug didn't work on me," replied Jasmine. "It seems the drug didn't work on you either."

Arnold laughed. "Not quite. They just didn't give it to me. You see I'm privileged."

"You're a lunatic, that's what you are!"

Arnold watched Tom struggle with his restraints.

"Why don't you go and say hello," said Arnold to Oliver.

Oliver raced to Tom and tore off the gaffer tape and ropes from his arms and legs.

Arnold proceeded to his desk and opened the bottom drawer.

"Now that everyone knows each other, there's only one thing to do," muttered Arnold, who retrieved the dirtied clothes and threw them onto the desk.

Jasmine gasped.

Arnold walked to his desk. "Yes, that's right. Seeing that you remember the past, you'd remember more than anyone the devastation that NIFA had on the entire world. Millions upon millions died, including many of our loved ones. Mr McPherson was very kind to us," he said, pounding his fist on the desk. "We started a new life here. Free of disease. Free of corruption. Life was great. Yes, we all wear the same clothes." Arnold removed his black cloak and hung it over the back of his chair. "Well, most of us do," he smiled. "But it's a small price to pay for what the Cooinda government provides us. We work for free and in return we acquire knowledge. What could possibly be better than that?"

"Why do we all wear the same clothes," asked Aurora.

Arnold pointed to Aurora's grey suit. "We like conformity. It's easier that way."

"Who's we?" Aurora asked with suspicion.

"The Cooinda government of course. Oh, you thought I was the government." He laughed again. "No, no, no. I'm more of an — advisory."

"Why did you come looking for me, Arnold?" asked Jasmine, looking around the room for an escape.

"Just to check on you of course."

Oliver finally removed the last of the restraints on Tom,

freeing him.

"Ah, good. I must have tightened them a bit too much, hey?" said Arnold, pointing to the discarded restraints.

Arnold reached into the drawer and retrieved a gun and pointed it between Tom and Oliver. "Right, enough talk. I saw you two enter the other night," he said waving his gun over the screens. "I saw everything. You shouldn't have come here. Why did you come here?" Arnold walked towards Tom, stopping short. "You're vermin, you two. You're nothing but diseased pests. Pests that need to be eradicated."

"Arnold," cried Jasmine. "I know how you're feeling. I experienced it too. But this isn't the answer."

Arnold turned to Jasmine and pointed it at her. "Isn't it? And tell me, Jasmine. Why shouldn't I kill you too? Do you realise the pain and misery you have caused?"

Barry raced into the room panting.

"Well, well. If it isn't Mr Protector. How's your leg, Barry? Still limping from that accident?"

Jasmine clenched her fists and screamed, "You fucking maniac!"

Arnold laughed. "She's a fiery one isn't she?" He stopped laughing abruptly and pointed the gun at Tom. "I've had enough of this." Arnold pulled the trigger and the 0.41 calibre bullet fired through the air and ripped through his chest."

"No!" yelled Oliver, and ran at Arnold.

Arnold weaved and Oliver's body struck Arnold's desk, sending him over the top. The tomato plant sailed off the desk and smashed onto the ground.

"No! Not my beloved green tomato plant," yelled Arnold.

Tom screamed in pain. "Ah shit!" he exclaimed, looking at his punctured chest. His shirt turned crimson and he began to wheeze.

Oliver got himself off the floor and ran to Tom's aid. "Stay with me, buddy. It's not your time yet," he sobbed. He looked towards Arnold. "What have you done? You're a lunatic."

Arnold didn't respond and aimed his gun at Oliver's head. Tom shook uncontrollably from shock.

"I think I'm done for, mate." cried Tom.

'No, you're not. Just stick with me," replied Oliver.

Tom's eyes rolled back into his head. The floor was a sea of blood.

"He's gone", muttered Arnold. "And now it's time for you to join him."

Arnold aimed at Oliver's head. Oliver anticipated Arnold pulling the trigger and ducked. The projectile whistled over Oliver's head piercing the window. Oliver quickly got to his feet and lunged towards Arnold, tackling him to the ground. The revolver came loose from Arnold's hand, landing about a metre away from the tackled pair. Oliver's brute strength allowed him to grip Arnold's neck, with a firm stranglehold. His jugular distended, as he gasped for air.

Barry limped towards the revolver but Jasmine held him back.

"Don't," she grunted. "We're getting out of here." She signalled to Aurora who was looking on in shock at the tussle on the floor. They slowly made their way towards the exit, but not before Arnold noticed them.

Arnold kneed Oliver's abdomen. He had managed to make contact with his diaphragm. Oliver instantly released his hold of Arnold's neck and held his stomach. Realising his temporary freedom, Arnold pounced onto the gun and established his aim. He fired his gun, with the bullet hitting Oliver right between the eyes. He died instantly.

Aurora let out a huge whelp. "No."

Barry lunged towards Arnold with his hands outreached.

Arnold fired again, this time into Barry's abdomen.

'You bastard,' yelled Barry.

Arnold dropped the gun from his hand and inspected the damage. Barry's thorax oozed and he slipped in and out of consciousness.

Jasmine ran towards Barry, cradling him in her arms and rocking him. "Please. Please. Don't leave me, Barry." She turned towards Arnold screaming, "You bastard. You fucking bastard. Why can't you just leave us alone?"

Barry's entire body quivered as he gasped for air.

"I love you, Jazz. I always have and always will!" said Barry whose colour faded from his face and his body went limp.

Aurora stood motionless in the middle of the room. She looked around the room. She sobbed upon seeing the bloodied bodies of Oliver and Tom and then gave out a blood-curdling scream when she saw her mother holding Barry's lifeless body. "Dad! Please! No!"

Arnold's face and clothes were drenched in sweat. He looked towards the exit, ready to escape.

Seeing the discarded gun on the floor, Jasmine picked it up and aimed it towards Arnold. She noticed an inscription on the barrel, *A*.

"Mum. Don't do it," Aurora pleaded. She didn't want to see any more death.

Jasmine kept her eyes fixed on Arnold. "I'm not going to kill him," replied Jasmine, through gritted teeth.

"Walk. Go to the tree," said Jasmine who indicated for Arnold to walk out of the building and into the garden.

They stepped out into the daylight.

"Up against the tree," yelled Jasmine. "Now!"

Some onlookers noticed the commotion and called the police. Within minutes sirens could be heard approaching the gardens.

"Open it," she instructed Arnold.

"You don't want to do this, Jazz."

"Don't call me that! And I said, open it!"

The onlookers could be heard gossiping amongst each other. "What is she doing?" one said.

"She's gone berserk," said another.

"Jasmine, we can talk about this," Arnold begged.

"Why did you come looking for me, Arnold?"

"Do you know how much hurt you've created?"

"How much hurt I've created? Are you kidding me?"

"You weren't supposed to be with Barry."

Jasmine took a step towards Arnold. "I swear to God if you don't open that door—"

"Mum, what are you doing?" asked Aurora, still in shock.

"Sending him to his death," snarled Jasmine.

Arnold took a pen-looking device from his pocket and pressed its top. In doing so, the doorway of the tree opened. There was an audible gasp from the onlookers.

Aurora was just as amazed by the door opening this time, as she was when the intruders appeared. "How did you know it could open?"

"I remember McPherson pressing that fob just before we entered here," Jasmine replied, not taking her eyes and gun off of Arnold.

"But how did you know he would have it?" Aurora pressed.

"Just a hunch," replied Jasmine. "Get in," yelled Jasmine to

Arnold.

"Jasmine. Please," pleaded Arnold.

"Now."

"I don't want to die."

"Too late for that."

Arnold dropped the pen from his hand and reluctantly stepped into the tree.

A shot rang out and the door of the tree closed.

Chapter 24

"Thanks for bailing me out, Matty", said Arnold to his brother.

"Hey! That's what brothers are for aren't they?"

Arnold hugged his brother and they left the Brisbane City Police lockup.

"Just tell me you'll leave Jasmine and her boyfriend alone, now?" smirked Matty.

Arnold grinned, "Of course, Matty! Hey, thanks for helping me out with the car."

Matty inspected his calloused hands. "I learnt only from the best." Both Matty and Arnold laughed.

"Come on let's go home," said Arnold.

Arnold got into his rusted four-cylinder car and cranked up the radio, his arm out the window, tapping his hands on the roof to the steady rock rhythm. Matty popped some tablets into his mouth and swallowed hard.

"You still sick Matty?" asked Arnold, looking over at the half-blistered pack in his brother's hand.

"Yeah," replied Matty. "I just can't rid this damn infection. I don't think this city air is good for me, either. I think I might head back out to our old stomping ground and find some work. What are you going to do?"

Arnold shrugged. "Be a pilot."

Matty took hold of his brother's arm, "You know you can't."

Arnold shrugged his brother's hand away, "No one can tell me I can't do something," he huffed.

"You're colour blind, Arnie."

"Don't you think I know that?" Arnold looked out the window into the cloudless sky. "Why is my life so screwed up?"

"Screwed up? What do you mean?"

"It's been screwed up since mum and dad died," said Arnold, smacking his hand on the steering wheel.

"God, I miss them."

Arnold's face went red, "Miss them?" he yelled. "Dad was a mean, old prick." His hands tightened around the steering wheel.

"But why mum?"

Arnold snarled at his brother. "Do you think I meant to? The bastard was laying into her. She just got in the way."

Matty wiped a tear from his eye. "We should have told the police the truth."

"The truth? Do you know what would've happened if we told them? We'd be locked up forever writing diary entries and trying to avoid being pummelled to death by the other inmates. I'm pretty sure Uncle Will wouldn't have bailed us out either."

"They would've understood that it was an accident."

"An accident? Killing dad wasn't an accident. That prick deserved everything he got."

"No, I mean, Mum."

Arnold took a deep breath. "It's in the past. What's been done, is done."

"What's with the chessboard and tomato bush?" asked Matty,

looking at the back seat.

"Souvenir."

"Where did you get the plant from, anyway?"

Arnold grinned. "He wasn't looking after it. The poor thing was sitting in the corner of his room, dying of thirst."

"Arnie, you're obsessed with her."

"She's meant to be with me!" he exclaimed. The car began to drift towards the left.

"Arnold, for fuck's sake."

Arnold adjusted the car back into the lane. Matty gave out a huge sigh.

"You trying to kill me now?"

"Relax." He turned up the radio on hearing, *There You Go*, by Pink. He sang along.

"You're completely tone-deaf," said Matty, shaking his head.

Arnold brought the car to a screaming halt, forcing cars behind him to hit their brakes. Loud screeches of tyres were heard down the freeway.

"Are you crazy?" screamed Matty.

"A little. I've got an idea."

"Yeah, I do too. Get this car moving again before that big burly bloke that's coming our way kills us."

"You and I could start a company."

"A company? You don't know anything about business."

"I know how to count," Arnold smiled.

"I don't think your obsession in counting in even numbers counts. What sort of business?"

"We procure scientific information and we sell it to pharmaceutical companies or research laboratories."

"But neither of us are scientists."

"I didn't say we do the work. We pay scientists to do it for us. We just cash in the rewards."

"Not a bad idea."

"And you thought I was crazy."

Matty laughed, "I still do."

Arnold outstretched his hand to Matty, "Let's make a pact."

"What sort of pact?"

"That we stick together, no matter what. We're brothers for life."

Matty took Arnold's hand, "Brothers for life."

Chapter 25

Word had quickly spread that Mike had abandoned the boys on the outskirts of town, leaving them for dead. There was even speculation that Mike may have gotten into a dispute with the boys, murdered them, and buried their bodies in a secret hideaway. Forensics obtained DNA samples from Mike just in case. Police combed his ute, revealing only a shovel. There was no evidence of blood or any biological sample other than plant sap.

The police next turned their attention towards the abandoned house. They went through each room finding bits and pieces that would interest only avid garage sale collectors. They even swept the acreage that the house was on. Nothing of interest was found, other than an old milking shed.

Detective Cooper stood in the open field with his arms folded."You find anything?" he asked Sergeant Jones.

"Nothing."

"What about that shed?" said Bill, pointing to a green tin shed that was hidden behind a giant fig tree.

"Nothing more than some hay bales and rusted milking equipment."

"There's something not right about this place," he lamented.

"Sir, my crew have been here two days straight now. They're

getting tired. I suggest we close this investigation down. Who knows, maybe they've left the outback and headed back home?"

Bill, who was over six feet tall, looked down over his subordinate. "You will stay here until I tell you otherwise. Is that clear?"

Jones straightened his uniform, pulling on his hem. "Yes, sir. Of course," he replied, walking back towards his patrol.

Bill stroked his chin and mumbled to himself. "They have to be here somewhere."

The sun was beaming and quickly warmed up the waterless ground.

"Bloody hell, this heat is brutal." Bill walked back towards the house and into the main bedroom to see if any progress had been made.

"You there?" said Bill to one of the constables. "What have you found?"

The constable held up a gas mask. "Only this, sir."

Bill snatched the mask from the constable's hand, inspecting it carefully.

"It's a gas mask, sir."

"Yes, I can see that. The question is, why is it here?" asked Bill. "How old were you ten years ago, son?"

"Me? Ah, about nine, sir." replied the constable, offering a grin.

Bill grunted and placed the mask down on the bed. "Do you remember NIFA?"

"NIFA? Oh, the virus. That's right, mum used to force me to wear face masks whenever we went out. Looked nothing like this though," said the constable, pointing at the gas masks. "Mum bought me this cotton mask that had huge teeth. All my friends laughed whenever they saw me wearing it."

"Thank you, constable."

"Oh, and don't get me started on lock-downs. How many did we have? I practically learned how to speak fluent French. Combien de temps jusqu' à ce que ce soit fini?"

"Constable! That is quite enough!"

The constable went quiet.

Bill looked disapprovingly at the young constable, before getting to his knees to look under the bed.

"Well! What do we have here?" replied Bill, grabbing the newspaper.

"January 2030, hey?"

"Does that mean anything to you, sir?"

"What's your name, son?" replied Bill.

"Simon Branson, sir."

"Where were you in January 2030? constable?"

"Ah, I went to Disneyland. Fantasyland was my all-time favourite."

"Enough!"

Bill got off the floor and sat on the edge of the bed, uplifting a plume of dust. "Let me know if you find anything." He scanned the room before the wall caught his eye.

"Odd," said Bill.

"What is, sir?" asked Branson.

Bill inspected the wall, palming the wallpaper as he did so. He found a small hole.

"Interesting," quipped Bill. "It looks like some sort of keyhole."

"We haven't found a key, though, sir."

"Hmm. Yeah, this is definitely a door of some sort. I can feel the outline of it."

"How do we open it?"

"Sledgehammer."

"Isn't that a bit drastic, sir?"

"You in charge here?" replied Bill, looking the constable up and down.

"No, sir."

"Right, call the office and get them to bring the hammer in ASAP."

"Yes, sir."

Another police vehicle arrived at the scene within the hour with the hammer.

"Right, knock down that wall," Bill instructed.

An officer pummelled the wall, revealing the passageway.

"Righto fellas. Who has a torch?" asked Bill.

Branson pulled out his torch from his kit belt.

"Right. Branson, you lead the way. I'll be right behind you. The rest of you follow behind. Is that clear?"

"Yes, sir!" came scattered responses.

Branson stepped through the doorway, looking back intermittently.

"Go on, son. You'll be right. We are all behind you," prompted Bill.

Branson swivelled the light all around. The light didn't penetrate very far in front of him and so short, hesitant steps were made down the stairway.

"Hello! Is anyone there?" called Bill. The only response he got back was that of his own.

"I'm not the best with small, dark spaces," said Branson.

They descended further and further down the passageway until Branson tripped.

"Ugh! What the heck is that?" let out Branson, lowering the torch towards the ground.

"What the hell?" said Bill.

In front of them was a body.

"Is he alive?" asked one of the officers standing behind the detective.

"Branson!" called Bill. "Check if they have a pulse."

Branson knelt and pressed his index and middle fingers on the body's carotids. After about a minute, he shook his head.

"How did it get here? And how long has it been here for?" asked Branson.

Bill crouched and inspected the body in the dimly lit passageway. "Not long by the smell of it."

"Should we move it to where there is more light, sir?" asked Branson.

"No!" yelled Bill. He took a deep breath. "No," he said more calmly. "We get forensics down here and they can do what they need to do before we move it. Is that clear?"

"Yes, sir," responded the group of officers.

The team ascended that passageway and waited for the town doctor and forensics team to arrive. Sometime later the team arrived.

"Detective, this is Dr Hargrave," introduced Sergeant Allsworth.

"The body is down there," replied Bill pointing to the passageway.

"Oh, I see. Well, we'll need some lights," said Allsworth. "Boys, grab the lights from the car," he yelled to his team.

The forensics team set up lights in the passageway and got to work.

The Sergeant donned an apron and fitted a pair of latex gloves and crouched beside the body. "Right, what do we have here then?"

The team began video recording and taking photos of the deceased from various angles.

"Looks like a gunshot wound," indicated Allsworth pointing at the body's face. "Half his bloody face is blown off."

His assistant busily scribed Allsworth's commentary.

Allsworth looked at the wall behind him and noticed a pear-shaped blood smear. "Odd." He looked up towards the entry. "It's as though he was shot at an angle."

"You think this is a homicide?" inputted Dr Hargrave.

Allsworth nodded. "Yeah, I'd say so. There's no weapon around here. Not even a shell."

The doctor took a thermometer out from his murder bag and took the temperature of the room as well as the body. "He's dead alright," he said as pressed the deceased's limbs. "Can't have been too long though. Rigor hasn't properly set in."

"Deceased is of male appearance. The body is lying on left lateral recumbent," said Allsworth. "Wearing a grey suit."

The group of police huddled around Bill and the body all drew in to take a closer look.

"Odd-looking suit to wear around Quilpie, don't you think?" said Dr Hargrave.

"No discernible tattoos or jewellery. Although there's a watch of some sort," noted Allsworth.

Allsworth inspected the body's wrist. "At least we now know his name."

"Sir?" replied Allsworth's assistant.

Allsworth turned the deceased's wrist, displaying the name ARNOLD SLATER.

"I've seen enough of what I need to see," said Allsworth. "Tidy this scene and bag the body when you're ready," he instructed his team. He discarded his gloves and gown onto the floor and walked up the passageway back into the main bedroom, along with Detective Cooper. "I think we're done."

"Great, thanks for coming out so quickly," replied Bill.

"Not a problem. We don't get many of these out here. We'll be in contact."

Bill nodded and walked out onto the veranda overlooking the grassed field. Branson joined him.

"What are you thinking, sir?" asked Branson.

Bill took a deep breath and replied; "There's something not quite right here. Who on earth is this?"

* * *

The Quilpie morgue was a very basic room, located on the bottom floor of the town's only hospital. The body was trolleyed into the room.

"Right. Shall we begin?" said Dr Hilston to his assistant.

He started with examining the body's gross appearance.

"The body is that of a well-nourished male. Age is unknown, but he appears to be middle-aged. There is no peripheral oedema of the extremities. There is an area of erythema on the right maxilla, congruent with an entry point of a gunshot wound. Conjunctiva shows haemorrhage bilaterally. There are no other scars evident."

The pathologist made an upside-down, Y-shaped incision starting at the top of the sternum.

"The right and left pleural cavities contain approximately thirty millilitres of clear fluid, with no adhesions. The heart is a normal shape and weight of four hundred grams. The pericardium is intact." Upon opening, the heart was grossly normal, except for the left ventricle, demonstrating a slight ventricle septum defect. "Most likely congenital I'd say," added Dr Hilston.

The pathologist continued the examination of the aorta, lungs, gastrointestinal system, reticuloendothelial system, genitourinary system, endocrine system, and extremities. No other pathology was evident.

"Right. Let's inspect his noggin," exclaimed Dr Hilston, amused by his humour. "Here's something you may not know. Did you know that the average person has about sixty-thousand thoughts a day? About 95% of them are the same thoughts you had the day before. Interesting huh?"

The assistant grunted behind his surgical mask.

The pathologist took a bone saw and cut through the body's skull.

"Good Lord. What a mess," said Dr Hilston. "Ok. The meninges have completely disintegrated! Ablation of the frontal and right parietal lobes."

Dr Hilston removed what was left of the patient's brain and inspected it, before weighing it.

"What do we have here?" said the pathologist. The assistant focused the overhead light onto the specimen in front of them.

"Well, that'll do it," exclaimed Dr Hilston, retrieving a bullet lodged in one of the body's sulci.

"Send this off to ballistics will you?" replied the pathologist, placing the bullet into a sterile specimen jar. "We'll send samples of his blood and brain to the lab to see if they can get a DNA profile on this victim."

After finishing up the examination, Dr Hilston began preparing the report to send to Detective Cooper.

* * *

At the police station, Detective Cooper ran through the day's events in his mind. The homicide still didn't sit well with him. He called Mike, to check on his whereabouts. The phone went through to voicemail.

"Hi, you have rung Mike. I'm either pruning the garden or have my head in a bonnet. Just leave me a message, and I'll get back to you."

"Hello, Mike. This is Bill Cooper here. Do you mind giving me a call back once you receive this message? Thanks."

Bill was feeling restless and decided to go back to the house.

The forensics team had left, leaving Bill alone. "Something's missing," he said to himself.

He inspected all the rooms, opening all the drawers and cupboards as he went. He entered one of the two other bedrooms. It was empty, except for a large wooden, hand-carved wardrobe and an unmade bed. The wardrobe was bare, other than a large A carved into one of the inner doors. He sat on the bed and looked out the window. *What am I missing?*

Bill left the house and took another breath in. One of the cows let out a low. Upon seeing Bill, it retreated away towards the old shed. Bill decided to follow the cow.

"Looks like it hasn't been used for a while," said Bill, looking at the discarded hoses and upturned milk vats. He noticed a door and turned the handle. "Locked. I thought the Sergeant said all he could see were hay bales?" He heard an engine from down the driveway. He turned towards the sound and noticed Mike's ute. "Mike, what are you doing here? I tried to call but you didn't answer."

"Oh, hi Bill. Sorry, I must have missed your call. I thought I might find you here," said Mike, getting out of his vehicle.

"So this is where you think the boys went missing hey?"

Bill shook his head and wiped the sweat from his brow. "Yeah, but we've got a new complication."

"Oh?"

"Yes, I can't say too much at this stage but perhaps you can assist?"

"Sure," replied Mike tucking his hands in his denim jeans.

"What did you want to see me about anyway?"

"See you about?" inquired Mike. "Oh, yes, Di told me she dropped the boys off the other night at the motel."

"Ok," replied Bill.

"Thanks, I'll follow that up." Bill shifted his weight onto his left leg. "You mean to say you came out all this way just to tell me that?"

"Ah, yeah. I thought it was urgent."

"You didn't think to give me a holler?"

"Ah, I was on my way to—."

"To?" Bill prompted.

"Ah, to look for the boys. I thought I might help you guys out."

"Really? Well, Mike, that's considerate of you."

Bill's phone rang. "Excuse me, I'll need to take this."

Bill spoke for half a minute whilst watching Mike wipe the dust off his car with his shirt.

"Ok, got it. I'll come back now," said Bill into his phone. "I have to go," he said to Mike. "You around later?"

"Sure, sure," replied Mike.

"Great. See you then."

Mike nodded.

Bill walked back towards the house, got into his car, and returned to town with the sun setting.

Chapter 26

"What just happened?" yelled Aurora. "What did you do?" she said, looking at Jasmine, the gun by her side.

The police sirens grew louder as they rounded the corner onto McPherson Parade.

"Quick! We have to get out of here. They find us and we're done for," exclaimed Jasmine, who tucked the gun into her pocket. "Go back to the building," she instructed.

"Are you serious?" responded Aurora. "I don't want to go back there."

"We need to get the remote for the car. It's in your father's pocket."

Jasmine picked up the fob that Arnold discarded, before running back to the McPherson building. They bounded up the stairs and entered the hallway on the third floor.

"What the—" gasped Aurora. "There's blood on the floor."

They followed the trail into Arnold's office.

Aurora was the first on the scene. "Where are the bodies?" she gasped. She anxiously looked around the room. "No, no, no! This can't be happening," she howled.

"We better get out of here. I think they know we're here," replied Jasmine, seeing the police enter the gardens.

"Let's go," said Jasmine.

"But how are we going to get out of here?" asked Aurora.

"I don't know, but we can't stay here," replied Jasmine.

They hurried out of the room into the hallway where they were met by Hayden.

"Hayden, what are you doing here?" inquired Aurora

"Oh, hi," replied Hayden, anxiously. "I was just helping my dad."

"Does he work here?" said Aurora.

"Ah, yeah, he is a security officer here," replied Hayden.

"Why are you wearing a black-zipped jacket?" queried Jasmine.

Aurora's mind flashed back to seeing Arnold, who was wearing a black cloak. She collapsed on the ground and sobbed.

"Are you ok?" Hayden asked Aurora.

Jasmine assisted Aurora to her feet. "Come on, love. We have to get going."

They heard footsteps coming from the stairwell.

"Shit, they're coming," said Jasmine.

"Who?" replied Hayden.

"There's no time to explain," replied Jasmine who looked for an alternative exit. "We're stuck."

"What about the elevator?" Hayden replied.

Aurora shook her head. "We don't have clearance."

"I do," replied Hayden.

Everyone looked at Hayden puzzled but had no time to question.

"Come with me," instructed Hayden.

They followed Hayden down the corridor in the opposite direction of the stairwell and found the elevator. He presented his wrist onto the scanner and the doors opened. They rushed in before the doors closed. Hayden pressed the car park level button. The elevator jolted and Aurora gave a short squeal. They all stared at the screen watching the levels slowly descend.

"Sorry, I'm Hayden," he said to Jasmine.

"I'm Jasmine, Aurora's mum," she replied.

"Glad to meet you."

There was an awkward pause.

"Nice day isn't it?" said Hayden. "Where are the boys?" he asked not taking his eyes off the screen.

The elevator reached the car park level and they shuffled out of the elevator.

"Now what do we do?" asked Aurora.

Hayden pointed to a car. "Get in. I'll drive."

They all looked at each other.

"Is there another way out of here?" asked Jasmine.

Hayden shook his head. "Afraid not."

Jasmine turned around to the elevator and noted that someone had activated the elevator.

"Ok," replied Jasmine.

"Mum," moaned Aurora.

"It'll be fine," whispered Jasmine.

Hayden summoned for the car from his wrist device. Within seconds the sound of a gentle hum could be heard approaching them. The car pulled up beside them

"Get in," Hayden called.

Jasmine hopped into the rear seat of the black-coloured vehicle. "Aurora, what are you doing?" she asked.

"I can't. I can't do this," replied Aurora, whose hands were shaking.

Jasmine got out of the car and gave her daughter a hug.

"Come on. We're in this together," she replied.

"We need to get going," Hayden called from the driver's seat, his voice reverberating off the granite walls.

Aurora reluctantly stepped into the hovered vehicle. She felt uneasy about the situation but knew she had little alternative. Jasmine sat next to her and closed the door.

Hayden commanded the car to go to City Hall.

"Why there?" asked Aurora, curiously.

"You wanted to get out of here, didn't you?" said Hayden.

The car exited the deep underground car park and made its way towards City Hall.

"Is this your car, Hayden?" asked Jasmine. She ran her hand over the soft polymer interior.

"Nah," Hayden laughed. "I just like to drive it. It's my father's."

"He's ok with you taking it?" asked Jasmine.

"Yeah, it'll be fine," replied Hayden. "I don't see much of him."

"He a busy man?" asked Jasmine who sat directly behind Hayden.

"You could say that," replied Hayden. "What you doing at the McPherson Building, anyway?" he said turning in his seat to face Jasmine and Aurora.

Aurora began to sob.

"She ok?" asked Hayden.

"It's just been a bad day for us," replied Jasmine.

"Who are you running from?" asked Hayden.

Aurora stopped sobbing to respond, "The police."

"The police?" replied Hayden, his eyes darting between Aurora and Jasmine. "What mischief have you two been up to then?"

"You have reached your destination," announced the car's navigation.

"Here we are," smiled Hayden.

They leapt out of the car before they were met by Crystal.

"Hey babe," said Hayden who kissed Crystal on the cheek.

"You remember everyone, don't you? Oh, this is Aurora's mum. Sorry I've forgotten your name," said Hayden.

"Jasmine," she said.

"Jasmine, yes, that's right," nodded Hayden.

"What are you two doing here?" asked Aurora who squinted.

There was a chime from the City Hall.

"Oh, looks like another death," frowned Hayden. "It also means that a lucky couple can apply for a baby and start getting busy," he grinned and cuddled Crystal.

Hayden locked the car. "What say we go in?" he said as he pointed to the City Hall.

"Ah, I think we might get going," replied Jasmine. "Thanks for getting us out of there."

Jasmine grabbed Aurora's arm.

"No, no, I insist," asserted Hayden. He looked around before surreptitiously pressing a stun gun into Aurora's back.

"Hayden, what are you doing?" asked Jasmine.

Crystal pressed a gun into Jasmine's back.

"I suggest you two keep it down and not make a scene unless you want to end up like the others," added Hayden.

Aurora's teeth started chattering.

Hayden combed Aurora's hair with his unarmed hand. "Oh, someone's a bit scared."

Aurora was so petrified she wet herself which she was embarrassed by.

"Don't worry about that. We'll clean up your mess, much

like the mess you left us already."

"Leave her alone," said Jasmine, her hands clenched.

"Come on, let's go inside where there aren't as many people."

Hayden and Crystal gestured for both Jasmine and Aurora to walk into the City Hall. They shuffled into the main atrium where only one other person sat on the couch awaiting their turn with the Divine. Hayden smiled at the lone visitor before proceeding into a darkened room.

"In there," Hayden instructed. He closed the door behind him and the lights automatically illuminated, revealing a row of glass chambered bodies.

Aurora gasped, "What is this?"

"All the deceased, of course," replied Hayden, removing the gun from Aurora's back and tapping it onto one of the chambers.

Aurora felt scared. She hated seeing death, especially when it was those that were close to her.

"Go on, take a look," gestured Hayden, down the hallway.

Aurora and Jasmine reluctantly stepped down the hallway with chambered bodies on either side of them. Aurora held onto her mother, not wanting to look at the lifeless bodies.

"God, this is like a shop of horrors," muttered Jasmine, with disgust.

Jasmine stopped and screamed, "Barry!"

Aurora unwillingly looked up at her father's body. She fell to the floor and pounded the floor. "No!"

"Your friends are there too," called Hayden from behind them.

Jasmine looked to the chamber next to Barry's. "What sort of disturbing place is this?"

"Where you'll be joining them," Hayden replied.

"You're a coward just like your father," scorned Jasmine.

Hayden laughed and looked at Crystal. "Do you hear that? She thinks I'm a coward."

Crystal joined Hayden in laughter.

"So, you've finally worked out who my father is then?" said Hayden.

Hayden's ACCESS vibrated. He answered, "Yes? Yes I know there's someone here for the Divine. Well, my father isn't here is he, so he can't answer the loser's questions. Tell him to come back another day. Tell him there's been a technical issue. I can't talk. Please don't disturb me again." He pressed his wrist device and looked at Crystal. "Can you believe these people? See what I have to work with?"

Crystal shook her head.

"Now, where was I?" Hayden continued.

"Where's McPherson? Or is he not real either?" scorned Aurora.

"McPherson? Of course, he's real. Have a look for yourself."

Hayden fiddled with his ACCESS before McPherson's chamber illuminated. "Ah, there's my great-uncle."

"But his holograms?" Aurora queried.

"Modern technology. Don't you love it?" laughed Hayden.

Hayden's ACCESS vibrated again. "What!" he answered. "Commotion? What sort of commotion? I'll be there in second."

Hayden pressed his wrist device and turned to Crystal. "There's something I have to take care of, make sure they don't leave here."

"Got it," replied Crystal aiming her gun at Aurora and Jasmine.

Hayden left the room, closing the door with a thud.

"Do you like your new home?" smiled Crystal.

Aurora walked towards Crystal. "Why are you doing this?" she asked. "You don't need to be a part of this."

"Shut up!" she barked.

"You're better than this, Crystal," added Aurora, drawing closer to Crystal.

"Stay back!"

"Why don't you let us go? We won't say anything to anyone." Aurora was now within a few metres of Crystal's outstretched arm.

"I'm warning you. I won't be afraid to use it."

"And I won't be afraid to use this!" exclaimed Aurora, activating her high-frequency alarm on her wrist device.

Crystal dropped the gun and covered her ears from the deafening sound. Aurora jumped to the ground and picked up the gun and aimed it at Crystal.

"Mum! Let's go!"

Jasmine ran to Aurora.

"Open this door," commanded Aurora.

Crystal threw her wrist device across the floor to Aurora. "Here, take it," she yelled.

Aurora pressed Crystal's wrist device to the door's scanner. The door opened and Aurora and Jasmine exited the room, closing the door shut behind them.

"Let me out," came a muffled call from the other side of the door.

They ran through the atrium, which was now crowded with hundreds of people, and outside into the fresh air.

"Aurora!" yelled Jake.

Aurora saw Jake standing by his car by the entrance. She and Jasmine ran to him.

"Thank Cooinda you're here." She gave Jake a hug. "I'm so, so, happy to see you," she whelped. She let go of him and looked into his eyes. "But how did you know we were here?"

"Crystal phoned me."

"Crystal?" replied Aurora, in shock.

"Yeah, she told me you two were in trouble."

"Maybe she wasn't a bad egg after all," Jasmine remarked.

Aurora felt a hint of empathy for Crystal's noble act.

"We need to get out of this city. Jake, are you able to take us to McPherson Gardens? The crowd should have left by now, hopefully."

Jake nodded.

They got into Jake's car and he commanded the car to McPherson Gardens.

"Did he hurt you?" asked Jake to Aurora, gently pushing aside Aurora's hair that was covering her face.

"No. But he would have, I'm sure, had he not left."

Jake smiled. "I might have had something to do with that."

Aurora looked up at Jake. "What did you do?"

"Let's just say I acted as a government official and told a heap of people that they could have free time with the Divine."

"Genius," replied Aurora.

They arrived at the gardens. It was nearing dark and the police and onlookers had left.

"To the tree," instructed Jasmine.

"What are you doing?" asked Jake.

"We're leaving. There's nothing more for us here. Besides if Hayden finds us, he will kill us," replied Jasmine.

"Come with us," insisted Aurora, taking hold of his soft hands.

"I can't," he replied. "I know nothing about this other place."

"Neither do I, but maybe seeing it again will jog our memories," replied Aurora, looking lovingly into Jake's eyes. "Please?"

"I haven't said goodbye to my family, though," said Jake, solemnly.

"We'll all be reunited again before too long, I'm certain," replied Aurora.

"Come on. Jake, if you're coming, you need to decide now."

Jake let go of Aurora's hands.

Aurora watched Jake walk away before leaning down to pick up one of the many flowers strewn across the synthetic ground.

"I'll keep this as a memento," smiled Jake and walking back towards Aurora. "Let's go."

Jasmine took the pen from her pocket and gave it one firm press. Nothing happened.

"No, no, no," cried Jasmine, feverishly pressing on the pen.

"Maybe the batteries are flat," remarked Jake.

Jasmine grunted at Jake.

"Why isn't this working," said Jasmine, with concern.

"Here," said Aurora, snatching the pen from her mother's hand. "Let me have a go."

Aurora pressed the pen once and the door of the tree opened. Jasmine looked at Aurora with frustration.

They stepped into the tree and stood motionless for a few seconds before the door closed.

Chapter 27

Bill rested one arm on the centre console of his electric-powered car. "Something's amiss with Mike," he said to himself. "He's been acting strange ever since I called him into the café."

Bill selected *Mike* from the phone menu in his car. The call went straight to message bank. "Damn!" exclaimed Bill who pounded his hand on the dashboard. He braked hard and spun the vehicle around and raced back to the old house. The day had turned into night. The high-beam lights, from his car, were swallowed from the moonless dark. When he arrived back at the old house, Mike's ute was nowhere to be seen.

Bill got out of his car. "Dammit. Where has he gone?" He looked around the deserted paddock and heard the door from the shed, banging in the light breeze. "Odd. That door was locked before." He removed his gun from its holster and held it close to his body and aimed at the ground. "Police! Anyone in there?" he called through the open door. His pulse raced and he felt a drop of sweat run down the back of his neck, even though it was now night. He held onto his breath as he stepped inside the room. "Bloody hell," he exclaimed.

Inside was a computer covered in dust, along with a single mattress. The walls were covered with photos of a young girl.

"What the hell is this?" said Bill who holstered his gun. "So much for only old milking paraphernalia and hay bales?"

He tapped on the keyboard and the screen came to life.

"God. How old is this thing?"

Bill attempted to recall how to operate the old computer. He moved the mouse to a folder titled, "Jasmine". Upon opening the folder, hundreds of photos of the same girl displayed on the walls popped up on the screen.

"Interesting."

He then selected "MAIL" from the home screen. The inbox was mainly empty other than several emails from William McPherson. Bill clicked on one of the messages.

Hello Arnold,

This virus is out of control. Thankfully we have built a new city that will be open soon. I am so happy that you and your son, Hayden have been selected to join us. We will ensure that no one escapes from the new city until it is safe to return. There's an alarm that has been installed should anyone try to re-enter from Cooinda. Can you please tell Matty this so that he can ensure no one enters? All measures must be taken to not allow anyone to re-enter Qulipie. He'll just have to check the alarm program I have installed on your computer regularly.

No one should be able to get into Cooinda either without the electronic fob I've left for you to give to Matty and the hidden pressure sensors in the passageway. The entry from the bedroom will automatically close after two minutes as a safety feature. Tell Matty that if the fob is lost, there's a button under the desk. Well, I think that's it. We will see you soon.

Your loving uncle,

William

P.S. My health hasn't been good recently. I suspect time is running out. I'll expect you to keep the place running when I depart. I've installed a fibre optic cable between here and Cooinda, so that you can communicate with Matty when you get there.

Bill put his hands on his head, realising the enormity of his discovery.

"Right. I better get this to the lab," he exclaimed.

Bill continued searching the room and found a gun lying on a bedside table. He glanced at it, without touching. "Interesting," he mumbled. He continued looking around the room but found nothing further of interest. He closed the door behind him. He pulled out his phone and selected *Forensics*.

"Hi, it's Detective Cooper here. Yes, can you please send out a crew to investigate the old house again? Yes, I know you've already been there. There's a shed about two hundred metres from the house that is hidden behind a tree. Yes, that's right, the one with the hay bales. Yes, I think it could be of interest. Thank you."

Bill got back into his car and drove back to town at full speed. "I need to find Mike."

Chapter 28

The next morning, Detective Cooper was awoken by one of the station's officers.

"Ah, excuse me, sir?"

Bill grunted and wiped the drool from the corner of his mouth. "Oh, ah, yes?" he replied, rubbing his eyes. "What time is it?"

"Almost seven, sir," replied the officer, looking at his watch.

Bill yawned, "God, I must have dozed off." He got to his feet and tucked his creased white shirt into his trousers. "Right, where are we at with Mike?"

"Is he a person of interest, sir?"

"God damn right he is," squawked Bill.

Another officer walked into Bill's office. "Sir, we have a report on that gun found at the old milking shed," replied Constable Anderson. Josh Anderson was a probationary officer, not long out of training.

"Yes?" said Bill.

Anderson handed Bill the forensics file which he flicked through. "Point four-one calibre hey? MIL Thunder Five? God' I haven't seen one of those for years. I bet you didn't see anything like this through your training, hey?" asked Bill to the young officer.

"Ah, no, sir."

"Sir, Dr Hilston is on the line for you," came a call outside of Bill's office.

"Ah! Thank you. Put him through to my office, would you?"

Detective Cooper sat back into his cushioned leather chair.

"God, I hate this chair," he lamented to no one in particular. "Why leather in a town like this?"

His phone rang once before he picked up the receiver.

"What did you find, doc?"

"Hello, detective. I'll send through the report in a few minutes, but I just wanted to let you know that we have established a cause of death."

"Yes?" interrupted the detective.

"Cessation of life as a result of a single gunshot wound. A point four-one calibre bullet was found lodged in the deceased's brain.

"Go on."

"Very well, sir. We have, of course, provided biological samples to the lab and are still awaiting results. I do, however, wish to share with you some intriguing information. Which is why I have called, in fact."

Detective Cooper reclined further in his chair, elevating his feet onto his desk. "Yes," he said, not overly intrigued as he'd seen a great deal in his illustrious career and was rarely surprised.

"Well, we submitted cheek, hair, and saliva samples for DNA analysis."

"Yes."

"We ran it through our database."

"Spit it out already, doc. It's like drawing blood out of a stone."

"The deceased matches an individual named Matty Slater."

Cooper dropped his feet off the desk, back onto the floor. "Are you sure? I have his wrist device that says, Arnold Slater."

There was a knock on the detective's door. "Sir, you're needed right away."

"Damn. Doc, sorry I have to go. I'll call you back in a jiffy," answered Bill, hanging up the phone.

"What could possibly be so urgent, Constable?" asked the detective.

"We have the results from the ballistics team, sir," replied the constable.

"Yes?" said Bill.

"The object retrieved from Mr Slater is a point four-one calibre suitable for a Bond Arms Texas Defender, Smith & Wesson Governor, D-Max Sidewinder, or a MIL Thunder Five."

Bill shifted his weight. "Wait. What was the last gun you mentioned?"

"Ah, the Thunder Five, sir?"

"Mike," exclaimed Bill.

"Mike, sir?"

The detective waved his hand. "Anything else?"

"The team test-fired the apprehended gun, and the marks are identical to the bullet retrieved from Mr Slater's brain."

"Hmm, you don't say?" replied Bill.

"The team was also able to sample gun powder residue, sir."

"Interesting."

"One more thing, sir. They analysed the trajectory, and it appears that the shooter was standing from atop the passage-way.

"Ok. I think it might be time to call in our lead suspect, don't you?"

"Who's that, sir?"

"Mike Hislop. You'll find him at the Quilpie Motor Inn."

"Roger that," replied the officer, moving into action.

* * *

Meanwhile, at the Motor Inn, Mike was packing the last remaining bags into his ute. He stood back and looked at the hedge, impressed with his horticultural skills.

"I'm going to miss this place," he said to himself.

"Mike," called out Cheryl. "You almost forgot your tomato plant."

Mike turned towards Cheryl, holding his beloved plant. It had produced a lot of fruit in its life. He smiled at her and replied, "It's ok, Chez. You can keep it."

"Oh, ok, sure. I know just the recipe for these babies," Cheryl replied. "We're sure going to miss you around here, Mike. But it sounds like Di has found a good job in the big smoke, hey?"

"Yeah, she only applied yesterday. Lucky thing. Anyway, I best get out of here and go find her."

Mike started the engine and gave it some juice. The roar resonated off the concrete walls of the hotel. "Well, goodbye."

"See ya!" said Cheryl, waving frantically.

Just as Mike began to drive out of the car park, three police vehicles cornered Mike's ute.

"Police!" yelled an officer.

Cheryl hugged the pot plant close to her, "Oh my goodness, what is going on?"

"Get out of the car!" yelled another officer, approaching

with his gun aimed at Mike's open window.

"Ok, ok," replied Mike, who raised his hands.

The officers slowly began to move in towards the ute.

"Put your hands on the steering wheel, where we can see them," yelled one of the officers.

Mike complied and shifted his hands onto the wheel. The officer's closed in, but not before Mike blew Cheryl a kiss and slammed his foot onto the accelerator. The ute jolted forward and smashed through the low-level, Besser-brick wall. The officers quickly jumped into their vehicles and gave chase. Mike spun the ute off Brolga Street onto Chipu Street, before making a hard right onto Kookaburra Street. The screech of tyres was deafening. He accelerated and went to turn onto Quarrion Street but misjudged the corner. Instead, the ute completed a three-sixty and smashed through the John Waugh Park fence. It finally came to a stop near the Quilpie Club. Mike's head impacted the steering wheel hard, rendering him unconscious. The police were not far behind and quickly ascertained that Mike had come off the road, judging by the tire marks and busted fence. They made their way by foot to the wreck, finding Mike slumped over the steering wheel.

"Mr Hislop. Mr Hislop. Can you hear us?" yelled the first responder, checking for a pulse.

"He's still alive!" he said to one of his colleagues. "Call an ambulance."

The crash had brought a crowd of people from the club, about to begin a night of line dancing.

"Ok, everyone, get back. This is a crime scene, now. Get back," yelled the officers.

Mike came to, groaning in pain. "Ugh! What happened?"

"It's alright, Mr Hislop, you've been in an accident. Just relax, and we'll get you out of here," replied the officer, cuffing his left hand to the steering wheel.

"We're going to take you to the District Hospital, as soon as the ambulance arrives, ok?"

Mike squirmed, desperate to escape, but it was no use. He wouldn't get very far in the state he was in. The sound of more sirens could be heard from the distance, and within a matter of minutes, they arrived at the scene. The paramedics applied a neck brace and carefully moved Mike onto the stretcher, into the ambulance.

"We will follow you to the hospital," said one of the officers to the paramedic.

The ambulance escorted Mike to the hospital, where he was cuffed and examined. After confirming no serious head injuries, he was transferred to the general ward, under police guard. The officers called the detective advising him that Mike was now in the hospital.

Detective Cooper wasted no time and raced to the hospital. He located Mike's room, flashing his identification to the officers securing the room, and entered.

"Good evening, Mike," said Bill.

Mike didn't respond.

"So, I thought I said to you not to skip town?"

No response.

"You do know you're now our prime suspect, Mike?"

No response.

"With your permission, I'd like to obtain a DNA sample from you."

Finally, Mike spoke. "I want a lawyer."

"Of course, Mr Hislop," replied Bill.

"I ain't saying another word until I have a lawyer by my side."

"Constable," called the detective, to one of the officers standing guard.

"Yes, sir," replied the officer.

"Can you please arrange a lawyer for Mr Hislop?"

"Yes, sir."

"Oh, and make it quick, hey? I have line dancing on tonight," quipped the detective.

The detective left the room temporarily and sat, browsing through his emails. One that caught his attention was titled 'AUTOPSY REPORTS FOR SLATER.' He opened the email, reading the detailed reports. 'Cause of death, ablation of respiratory centres and medulla oblongata, as a result of a penetrating wound from a foreign object.' He continued browsing. As he was doing so, a new email arrived. 'DNA ANALYSIS ON SLATER.' He selected the email and read the report.

The phone slipped out of his hand, landing on the floor and smashing the screen. As he leaned down to pick up his phone, a pair of shiny black leather shoes came into the detective's field of view. He stood up and was faced with a tall, lanky, man holding a briefcase. The stranger offered his hand.

"Good evening, I'm Jackson Lawson, from Lawson and Associates."

Detective Cooper shook his hand. "Glad you could make it here so promptly, Mr Lawson. Your new client is in room 12 A," pointing down the hallway.

"Very well. I will be a few minutes and will call you in when I'm ready."

After about ten minutes, Mr Lawson called the detective into the room. "Ok, my client has agreed to provide a DNA sample, on the proviso that he be let free."

"I'm afraid I can't do that, Mr Lawson. Your client is our prime suspect."

"But you have no evidence, no motive, nothing."

"That's not quite true, Mr Lawson. We're still working on his motive, but we have evidence in the form of a weapon, allegedly used in the crime. I should add his alibi is pretty damn flimsy too."

Mr Lawson turned towards Mike.

"I'd like a word with my lawyer please, Bill," said Mike.

"Sure thing. Take all the time that you need," replied the detective, with a smile on his face.

After a few minutes, Bill was called back into the room.

"My client has agreed to provide you with a DNA sample, detective."

"Thank you."

Bill smiled without saying another word and left the hospital, to return to the police station. He opened the database of missing persons, entering the year 2030. Thousands of names scrolled up the screen. He entered *Slater* into the database.

"Well, I'll be!" said the detective.

ARNOLD SLATER

"What on earth is going on here?" he said to himself. "How is it that all these people have supposedly succumbed to the pandemic and then all of a sudden, we find one of them at the bottom of a passageway in an abandoned house?"

The detective swivelled in his chair and looked up at the ceiling for inspiration. "Something is missing here. And I bet it has something to do with Mr Hislop."

His desk phone rang.

"Hello?" answered Detective Cooper.

"Ah, hello, detective. This is one of the scientists from the molecular biology lab."

"Yes?"

"We have obtained a sample from Mr Hislop, and have we have ran a rapid PCR analysis on it."

"Yes?"

"Well, we then entered the sequence data into our database."

"Oh for goodness sake, what is it with you lab people? Just spit it out"

"Yes sir, well, the sequence matches with an individual named Arnold Slater."

"Slater, did you say?"

"Yes, a Mr Arnold Slater, sir."

The phone went dead.

"Sir? Sir? Hello?"

Chapter 29

The passageway fell into darkness.

Aurora screamed, "I can't see."

Jasmine held onto her daughter's hand. "It's ok, I'm here with you."

"Jake? Jake? Where are you?" she cried.

"I'm here too," replied Jake.

"Where's your hand?" asked Aurora.

Jake felt for Aurora's hand in the dark.

"I'm scared." Aurora sobbed.

Jake switched on the light from his wrist device, illuminating the look of fear on Aurora's pale face.

"It's ok, Aurora," said Jake, giving Aurora's hand a squeeze.

"No! It's not ok!" Aurora exclaimed. "I watched three people be brutally killed, including my father, by a crazed monster. I've been kidnapped and had a gun pointed at my face. Now I'm stuck in this hole of a tree with no escape. It's not ok. Ok?" She broke down and cried.

Jasmine put her arm around her. "Oh, honey."

"And aren't you upset that dad was killed?" added Aurora, her sorrow changing to anger.

"Of course I am. I'm heartbroken, but I also know we need to get out of here."

"Ah, guys, sorry to interrupt but where's Arnold?"

"Jake, show me the floor," instructed Jasmine.

Jake shone his light onto the dusty stoned floor.

Jasmine gasped. "He's not here."

"What do you mean he's not here?" said Aurora, frantically. "Where is he?" Aurora was hysterical and started hyperventilating.

"Just calm down," Jasmine asserted. "We need to find a way out of here and then we'll find where Arnold went. But I need you to pull yourself together. Do you hear me?"

Aurora slowed her breathing and closed her eyes.

"I need you to tell me you're in control, Aurora," said Jasmine, pressing on her shoulders.

Aurora nodded.

"Good."

They heard footsteps.

"Help! Help!" yelled Jake.

"Jake, stop," called Jasmine. "If they hear us they'll probably kill us."

"Kill us?" replied Aurora.

"Calm down. If we stay quiet they won't know we're here," replied Jasmine, putting her hand across Aurora's mouth.

The steps stopped.

"See, they've gone," whispered Jasmine.

A light from the top of the passageway shone in their direction.

"Who's there?" said a deep booming voice.

They didn't move.

"I'm Detective Cooper from the Quilpie Police. Identify yourselves."

Jasmine gasped again. "Qulipe," she muttered.

Aurora was petrified. She was ready to wake up from this nightmare. And when she awoke, she'd be sitting in the comfort of her own home watching television with her father.

"Very well, I'm coming down then," said Bill.

Bill descended down the stairs towards them. With every step, Aurora felt her throat increasingly tightened. She closed her eyes.

"Who are you?" he asked again, the blinding light alternating between the trio.

"I'm Jake," he quivered.

"And you?" Bill asked, pointing his light at Jasmine's face.

"Jasmine, sir."

"Jasmine?" said Bill, taking a step closer. "There are photos of you sprawled all over a wall."

"What?" replied Jasmine.

"Long story. Remind me to tell you." Bill moved his torch to Aurora.

"What's your name, miss?"

Aurora stuttered and was unable to form words.

"This is my daughter, Aurora," replied Jasmine. "She, we, have all had a very traumatic day."

Bill sighed. "Come on. Let's get you guys out of here, hey?" he said, offering his hand.

Jasmine took hold of his hand. "Come on, let's go. I trust him," she said to Aurora and Jake.

Bill climbed the steps, with Jasmine, Jake, and Aurora closely behind. They arrived in the main bedroom of the house.

Jasmine looked around and covered her mouth with her hand, giving a short squeal.

Bill focused his torch on Jasmine. "Everything ok?"

"This place, I know this place?" replied Jasmine.

"You do?"

"Yes, ten years ago. I remember this place."

Bill shone his torch onto Jake and Aurora's faces. "What about you two? Do you remember this room?"

They both shook their heads.

"Why do you remember it then?" quizzed Bill to Jasmine.

"That's also a long story. Remind me to tell you," she smiled.

Aurora's feeling of fear subsided with her mum's familiarity with the place.

"Where's Arnold?" asked Jasmine.

Bill looked all three up and down. "Right now I need you to come with me to the morgue to identify him. Come on, come with me. I'll take you to the hospital."

"We didn't do it, you know," Jasmine added.

"I know," smiled Bill. "Come on," he said, gesturing towards the exit.

They crammed into the back seat of Bill's car.

"One of you can sit in the front with me, you know?" said Bill.

"It's ok, we'd rather stick together," replied Jasmine.

Bill drove the car down the darkened driveway with Aurora and Jake staring out the windows.

"Wow," said Aurora, in amazement of the starry sky. "It's so pretty. What are they?"

Bill looked back in the rear vision mirror to see what Aurora was looking at. "What? The stars?"

"Similar process to your science experiments with fruit, Jake," smiled Jasmine.

"If you say so," replied Jake.

"There's so many," added Aurora, in astonishment.

"Aha," replied Bill. "Trillions and trillions of the gas balls spanning an infinite universe. No one is really sure if it it continues or if it wraps on itself."

They passed a paddock with animals grazing in the dark.

"What's that?" asked Jake.

"They're animals," replied Bill. "Don't you have animals?"

"How much further?" asked Jasmine.

"Just around the corner," replied Bill. "So you escaped from here, hey?" asked Bill, turning his head to get a better view of Jasmine. "How?"

"Another long story," replied Jasmine, massaging Aurora's hand.

Jasmine nodded. "What happened to NIFA?"

"NIFA?" replied Bill, returning his attention back to the road. "Oh, God. I'll explain everything later," replied Bill as he turned into the hospital entry.

The detective led the new arrivals towards the hospital entrance and located the morgue, located on the basement floor. He opened the doors to the vacant morgue. A row of large refrigerators displayed the names of its occupants.

"Ok, here we go," said Detective Cooper.

The detective opened the door labelled 'Slater.' The drape was removed, and the body was revealed.

"Do you recognise this person?"

Aurora gasped. "What happened to his face?"

"Yes, I'm afraid the bullet did quite a bit of damage," replied Bill.

"A bit?" exclaimed Jake.

Aurora ground her teeth in anger.

"Yes, that's him," said Jasmine.

Aurora punched the lifeless body, hard in the abdomen. "You bastard! You stole my father. You bastard."

Jake restrained Aurora with difficulty. Jasmine assisted in bringing her under control.

"Aurora! Calm down," exclaimed Jasmine.

Aurora cried. "How could he?"

"Are you sure it's him? insisted Bill.

"Yes, that's Arnold," replied Jasmine, pointing towards the dorsal aspect of his left hand. "I have never forgotten that scar."

Bill took the deceased's hand and took a closer look. He then pushed the body back into its shelf, closing the door. "I know this must be hard for you."

"You have no idea what damage this man has done to me," said Jasmine, her voice wavering.

"I just want you all to meet someone if that's ok?"

"Who?" said Jasmine.

"Come with me," replied Bill.

* * *

Bill pressed the elevator button. After a short while, the doors opened and the rode the elevator to the first floor, where they disembarked. He led them down the hallway to room 12 A. He presented his identification to the officers, who moved aside. "Just you, Jasmine," he instructed. "One of the officers will look after you two."

"Hello Mike," said Bill.

Jasmine was confused. "Arnold?" she said.

Mike looked towards Jasmine. "Hello Jasmine"

"But, I just saw you," Jasmine gibbered.

The detective smiled. "Mr Slater, I think you have some explaining to do, don't you?"

"I don't need to explain nothing, Bill," said Mike.

Detective Cooper took hold of Mike's left hand, revealing a scar identical to the one Jasmine had just witnessed on the body in the morgue.

"What is going on here?" exclaimed Jasmine.

The heart monitor attached to Mike beeped faster and entered a tachycardia, setting off alarms. Medical staff scrambled into the room, shoving both Bill and Aurora out of the way. One of the nurses turned to the detective and said, "I think it's time for you to go now."

"Very well," replied the detective. "We will be back."

The detective and Jasmine left the room, but they remained within earshot of Mike.

"I know this has been a traumatic night for you. I think you should maybe all stay with me tonight. I'll have one of my officers take you there. I'm going to try to find the pathologist and see if I can glean any more details on the case."

"Officer," called the detective. "Take these three to 47 Galah Street, would you? Make sure they're settled in. You'll find a spare key just underneath the old tire by the front door."

The detective then turned his attention to the other officer guarding the door.

"Can you do me a favour? Can you go to the vending machine and pick up a bottle of water for me? I prefer bottled water than the sulphur tasting garbage we have here."

With his instructions delivered, the detective left the floor and took the stairs to the basement. Jasmine, Aurora, and Jake were escorted into the police vehicle and driven to the address Detective Cooper had provided.

"Right, let's get you inside and settled in," said the officer.

The key was located in the tractor tire as instructed, and the officer opened the front door.

"Nice place," said the officer, taking in the well-furnished lounge room. "I had better get back to the hospital. Is there anything else you need?"

"Ah, no, thank you," replied Jasmine.

"No problem. I'll see you later," said the officer.

The officer got into his vehicle and made his way back to the hospital to guard Mike.

It was now late into the night and Jake inspected the fireplace. "What's this?" he asked.

"You put logs in it and light a fire to keep the house warm" replied Jasmine.

"Fire? Logs?" replied Jake, picking up a piece of timber.

"Yes, those are logs. Can you maybe see if you can find some outside and I'll show you how to get this fire going. It gets cold out here during the night," replied Jasmine.

"Mum, I might go have a shower," said Aurora, who looked exhausted.

"Sure thing, love."

Jake went outside in search of logs, while Aurora freshened up. Jasmine collapsed into the sofa in the lounge room before she heard tapping. It was coming from the kitchen.

Her heart raced. She stood up and surreptitiously walked towards the kitchen. Her legs felt like lead. She could feel her entire body tensing. She attempted to call out for help, but she was so petrified that nothing came out. Through a concerted effort, she managed to walk to the kitchen where she saw a familiar face.

"Shh, " whispered Mike, still dressed in his hospital gown. "I'm not here to hurt you."

"Get out" yelled Jasmine. "Who are you? You're supposed to

be dead."

Mike walked towards Jasmine with a tear running down his cheek. "Do you know how long I've waited to see you again?"

"Get away from me. You hear?" yelled Jasmine.

"How's Barry?"

"You sick bastard."

Jasmine was completely confused and looked around the kitchen looking for something to defend herself with. She saw a large knife block, but it was on the other side of the room.

"We could play a little game," smiled Mike. "You remember how to play chess don't you?"

"Get back."

Mike held out his hand revealing a hand-carved chess piece. "Here, I made you another one."

"Mum!" yelled Aurora, standing in the lounge room with only a towel around her.

"Aurora, stay where you are!"

"So, you have a daughter, hey?" said Mike, smiling.

Mike continued walking towards Jasmine, forcing her to retreat into the lounge room where Aurora stood.

"Mum! What is going on?" called Aurora.

Jasmine raced towards Aurora and held onto her.

"Aurora, did your mother ever tell you about me?"

"You leave her out of this," grunted Jasmine.

Jasmine and Aurora reached a wall and were trapped in a corner.

Mike took hold of Jasmine's hair and sniffed. "God, I've missed you," said Mike with his eyes closed.

Jasmine and Aurora stood still. Jasmine's hands shook.

They heard a sound coming from the front door. Mike forced Jasmine and Aurora into the lounge room. The door opened and Detective Cooper entered the lounge room, holding his gun by his side.

"Good evening again, Mike. Or should I say, Arnold?"

Arnold became agitated. "I only came here to see Jasmine."

"Why, Arnold?" asked Bill.

"I don't understand what's going on here," sobbed Jasmine. "I thought Arnold was dead? I saw him. You showed me. He's dead"

"Why don't you tell her, Arnold?" grinned Bill.

All four sat down at the kitchen table. Arnold played with his wrist band. Jasmine noticed the name of 'Mike Hislop'.

"My name is Arnold Slater. I knew your mother very well, Aurora," said Arnold not taking his eyes off Jasmine. "I have always loved your mother."

"Stop it!" exclaimed Jasmine, smacking her hand on the wooden table.

"Ten years ago, we were in the middle of a pandemic," Arnold continued.

"Yes, yes, I know the story now. It was bleak; it caused mass death," replied Aurora.

Arnold interrupted her, "Yes, and so there was a secret ballot that my uncle held and I was selected to enter a newly established city."

"Wait, your uncle is William McPherson?" inquired Jasmine.

Arnold nodded. "Anyway, as I was saying before I was rudely interrupted. It was promised that we would be starting a new life. My twin brother had a disease. He has cystic fibrosis. I won't bore you with the details, but suffice to say that he had a lot of trouble in fighting off infections. I loved my brother. He was the only family I had left." Arnold looked towards the floor. "That is, other than my son, Hayden."

"Hayden? You mean that back-stabbing, childish, freak that tried to kill us?" asserted Aurora.

Arnold shifted his attention to Aurora and laughed. "I guess he's taken after his old man. I hope Matty took good care of him for me?"

"What does any of this have to do with your brother?" insisted Bill.

"I wanted him to live a life free of infections. If he stayed here, he would have worsened and probably died and so I swapped my identification with his. He went on, along with thousands of others, and entered a new life. I changed my name and I got on with living mine."

Arnold ripped off the nametag and threw it onto the floor.

"That's very altruistic of you Arnold," said the detective.

"So if you're Arnold, who's the guy in the morgue?" asked Aurora.

"My brother, Matty, of course," yelled Arnold. "I gave him my gun and my tomato bush." Arnold thumped the table with his fist. "Well, that was the plan."

"But the scar?" replied Jasmine.

"We both have the same scar. We're not only brothers but blood brothers too," replied Arnold.

"What about the boys, Mike?" said Bill, shaking his head. "I mean, Arnold."

"I have no idea what happened to them. Honest, Bill," replied Arnold, still focused on Jasmine.

"They're dead," said Aurora, with sorrow. "They intruded into Cooinda," she added.

"That means they must have somehow found the secret passageway," said Arnold, tapping his fingers on the table. "But how? They must have found the key."

"Where was the key?" asked Bill to Arnold.

Arnold looked at his feet, "I lost it. It must have fallen out of my pocket."

Aurora noticed the look of frustration on Arnold's face, but had no empathy for him.

"So how did you get in, Arnold?" asked Bill.

"There's a safety release in the shed. I was checking my work on the computer—"

"You mean fraudulently selling Cooinda's information to third parties?" interrupted Bill.

Arnold's face went red. "Do you know how much planning went into this? Do you?" he insisted.

"I suggest you calm down, Mr Slater," replied Bill. "Continue."

"Then the intruder alarm sounded. I pressed the button under the table and ran as fast as I could.

"And you shot your brother!" yelled Bill.

Arnold uplifted the table, the sound of timber smashing onto the ground, was deafening.

Aurora grabbed her mother's hand, fearful of Arnold's behaviour.

Arnold stood and calmly reset the table and resumed his seat. "He wasn't supposed to be there," he muttered.

"How did the boys die?" asked Bill to Jasmine.

"His brother killed them," replied Jasmine.

"I told them him to," smiled Arnold. "It had to be done. We couldn't risk them potentially infecting the entire city."

"You mean you and your family affair couldn't risk losing your scientific slaves?" grumbled Bill.

Aurora stood up, her chair smacking the ground. "You're all psychopaths! The whole lot of you!"

"Aurora! Please," said Bill, attempting to calm her. "So let me get this straight. The boys somehow found a way into this new city and then Arnold, or Matty in this case, killed them?"

Aurora and Jasmine both nodded.

Bill scratched his head. "And I'm assuming the passageway was the entry point for them?"

Aurora and Jasmine both nodded again.

"They came out of the tree," Aurora added.

"A tree?" replied Bill, inquisitively.

Arnold's bottom lip quivered. "I loved my brother. Why did he want to leave?" he insisted.

"I forced him to leave," replied Jasmine. "He killed the intruders along with my beautiful Barry."

Arnold leapt over the table, knocking his chair over in the process, and grabbed hold of Jasmine's throat.

"Let go of her, Arnold," exclaimed Bill who wrapped his hand around Arnold's hand.

Arnold released his grip. Bill retrieved one of the old photos of Jasmine that he had found in the old storeroom and threw it onto the table.

Jasmine massaged her neck as she struggled to breath.

"Well done, Detective Cooper!" replied Arnold, picking up the chair and resuming his seat.

Bill pointed to the photos. "It seems you have had a secret admirer for some time, Mrs Jemmerson."

Jasmine's body tightened as her mind flashed back to her time at university upon first meeting Arnold. Then seeing Barry in hospital. Followed by meeting who she thought was Arnold in Cooinda.

"Why did you send your brother to spy on me and my daughter?" asked Jasmine, sobbing.

"To finish the job I should have done a long time ago," he smiled.

Bill then threw the family photo onto the table. "The Slater family," announced Bill.

"There's just one thing that's missing."

"What's that?" asked Arnold.

"Your parents," replied Bill. "What happened to your parents?"

Arnold's hands formed fists and he started counting in even numbers, "Two, four, six, eight—"

"Arnold?" Bill pressed.

"Stop! Don't interrupt me!" Arnold rocked in his chair. "He was a maniac."

"Maniac?" scoffed Jasmine. "I'll tell you who's the maniac around here."

"Mrs Jemmerson, please," said Bill calmly.

"He hurt us." Arnold said, in rage.

"Well, Mr Slater, I think we've heard enough from you for the time being. Officers are waiting outside to escort you to your new home, where you'll be living for a very, long time."

Jake walked into the lounge clutching a handful of logs. "Whoa! What's going on here? Did I miss anything?"

Chapter 30

The next morning, Aurora walked into the kitchen, still at the detective's home. The detective handed her a mug of coffee.

"There you go," he said.

"Thanks. Where's Arnold?"

"I took him to the station. He's locked up for now."

Aurora noticed the sun's light streaming through the glass-pane window.

"Whoa, what's that light?" asked Aurora.

Bill looked out the window and smiled. "The sun."

Aurora walked to the window and felt its radiant heat. "What does it do?"

"It provides warmth, light, and energy."

"Like the Source," replied Aurora, in awe.

She heard the cawing from a crow, sitting on the barb-wired fence, outside the window. "What is that thing?"

Jasmine walked into the room.

"Morning, Mrs Jemmerson," said Bill.

"Please, call me, Jasmine."

"Morning, Jasmine. How did you sleep?"

"I didn't," replied Jasmine.

Bill nodded, "Yes, I suspect it will take some time for all of this to sink in."

"Mum, mum," called Aurora, in excitement. "Look what's here?" she said pointing to the crow.

Jasmine came over to the window and looked out. "Yes, that's a crow. They're pests."

"What can I get for you to eat?" said Bill who stood and opened the fridge. "I only have vegetables. I could make an omelette?"

Jasmine laughed, "That'll be fine, thanks."

"I'll go to the butcher later, today."

"Butcher?" replied Aurora, still taking in the outside world.

"They kill animals for food here, Aurora," replied Jasmine.

Aurora turned and faced her mother. "They kill? For food?" Aurora's stomach turned. "How could they do that? That's so—"

Jasmine shrugged, "Just the way it is."

Bill's mobile rang on the table. "Hello? Yes, I'll be right in." He placed the phone back onto the table, before saying, "I have to go into the station. Tidy up some loose ends on Mike, or Arnold, or whoever the heck he is."

Aurora curiously looked at Bill's phone. "Is that how you communicate?"

Bill picked up his phone. "This? Oh, here I'll take a photo of us, if that's ok?"

"Sure," replied Jasmine.

Bill took a selfie shot of himself, along with Aurora and Jasmine. "I'll post it on Facecatalogue."

"What is that?" asked Aurora.

Bill laughed, "I'm guessing you didn't have social media either?"

Jasmine shook her head.

"Probably not a bad thing, truth be told. Don't know

who's watching and using other people's information. Oh, which reminds me, I think you might find something rather interesting. Come with me, I want to show you something."

Aurora looked at her mother to ascertain if it was safe to do so. Jasmine gave an approving nod.

"I'll go wake up Jake," said Aurora, walking towards his bedroom.

"No, no, he can sleep here, I'll leave a note to say we're out and I'll give him a spare mobile to contact me on if he's concerned. We'll grab a bite on the way. The bakery here has the best brekkie rolls in all of Queensland, I reckon."

Bill scribbled a note to Jake and placed it on the kitchen table along with a spare mobile phone, before taking a sip of his lukewarm tea. "Let's go," he instructed.

They drove through the town, the weatherboard houses clearly visible in the morning sun.

"These houses, they're so—"

"Old?" replied Bill, giving a chuckle.

"Different," replied Aurora.

"I'm starting to sense that."

They arrived at the bakery.

"Hi, Denise. Say hello to my new friends, Jasmine and Aurora," said Bill, perusing the cabinet for food to eat.

"Hi, there," replied Denise. "You two from out of town?"

Jasmine smiled, "You could say that. We haven't been here for a while."

"Yeah, Nah, nothing hasn't changed much. What would you like this morning, Bill?"

"Grab me three of your delicious brekkie rolls, Denise."

"Sure thing."

Denise prepared the rolls and punched her fingers on the

cash register.

"What is she doing?" whispered Aurora to Jasmine, in astonishment.

"They have to pay for the food."

"With what?"

"It's called money. People receive money for the work they do."

"What about knowledge?"

"It's freely available."

Aurora watched the transaction in amazement.

"Thanks, Denise, have a great day."

"You too."

"Let's get going," added Denise to Jasmine and Aurora.

They pulled into the station.

"Follow me," instructed Bill.

They followed Bill into the station, where there was one officer playing a computer game in the corner of the room, and the other officers leaning on desks, conversing with each other. As soon as they entered the room, activity ceased and the officers stood to attention.

"Morning, sir," said one of the officers.

Bill didn't respond and strolled to his office and closed the door behind Aurora and Jasmine.

"Take a seat," he commanded, pointing to two vacant seats.

Aurora and Jasmine sat and patiently waited while Bill pulled out a bulging manilla folder from the filing cabinet.

"Right, here we are," smiled Bill. "Seems that you guys have been busy."

"Busy?" remarked Aurora.

"Yeah, we examined the computer that was located in a shed beside the house where you arrived last night.

"Some interesting info, I have to say. As you know, Arnold and Matty are nephews of William McPherson."

Both Aurora and Jasmine nodded.

"It seems that the brothers have been using you all. They've been using your skills and research for their own financial reward."

Aurora was concerned. "They were using us?"

"The Divine," muttered Jasmine. "They made us think we were doing work for knowledge."

"Yes," replied Bill. "But they were then selling your data and information to scientific companies, who would then pay the brothers rather handsomely."

Aurora was furious. "How could they?"

"I guess with every society there are pros and cons," said Bill, waving his hand around the room. "We're still stuck in 2030. At least your city has flourished. I think it might be time to reunite."

What was the name of the city you were from?"

"Cooinda," Aurora remarked.

"Cooinda, sounds like a 'Happy Place.'"

About the Author

Mark Street is the author of the debut book, The Intruders. He has acquired a Bachelor of Science and Masters in Science degree and worked as a senior scientist for a number of years, before turning his attention to aviation, where he works as a professional airline pilot. He is also a music composer for a number of films and TV episodes; and co-founder of a successful multi-sports and mindfulness company. He is currently in his final years of medical school.

Mark is the husband to wife, Tamara, and father of two young boys, Ashton and Zavier. When not working, he enjoys spending time with his family and travelling.

You can connect with me on:

http://www.markstreetcomposer.com

https://www.facebook.com/MarkStreetWriter